EMISSARY

PROTECTORS
UNDERCOVER
—TEAM ONE—

BOOK TWO

USA TODAY BESTSELLING AUTHOR

HEATHER SLADE

MORE FROM AUTHOR HEATHER SLADE

BUTLER RANCH
Kade's Worth
Brodie's Promise
Maddox's Truce
Naughton's Secret
Mercer's Vow
Kade's Return
Butler Ranch Christmas

WICKED WINEMAKERS
FIRST LABEL
Brix's Bid
Ridge's Release
Press' Passion
Zin's Sins
Tryst's Temptation

WICKED WINEMAKERS
SECOND LABEL
Beau's Beloved
Coming Soon:
Cru's Crush
Bones' Bliss
Snapper's Seduction
Kick's Kiss

ROARING FORK RANCH
Coming Soon:
Roaring Fork Wrangler
Roaring Fork Roughstock
Roaring Fork Rockstar
Roaring Fork Rooker
Roaring Fork Bridger

THE ROYAL AGENTS
OF MI6
Make Me Shiver
Drive Me Wilder
Feel My Pinch
Chase My Shadow
Find My Angel

K19 SECURITY
SOLUTIONS TEAM ONE
Razor's Edge
Gunner's Redemption
Mistletoe's Magic
Mantis' Desire
Dutch's Salvation

K19 SECURITY
SOLUTIONS TEAM TWO
Striker's Choice
Monk's Fire
Halo's Oath
Tackle's Honor
Onyx's Awakening

K19 SHADOW OPERATIONS
TEAM ONE
Code Name: Ranger
Code Name: Diesel
Code Name: Wasp
Code Name: Cowboy
Code Name: Mayhem

K19 ALLIED INTELLIGENCE
TEAM ONE
Code Name: Ares
Code Name: Cayman
Code Name: Poseidon
Code Name: Zeppelin
Code Name: Magnet

K19 ALLIED INTELLIGENCE
TEAM TWO
Coming Soon:
Code Name: Puck
Code Name: Michelangelo
Code Name: Typhon
Code Name: Hornet
Code Name: Reaper

PROTECTORS
UNDERCOVER
TEAM ONE
Undercover Agent
Undercover Emissary
Coming Soon:
Undercover Savior
Undercover Infidel
Undercover Assassin

THE INVINCIBLES
TEAM ONE
Decked
Edged
Grinded
Riled
Smoked

THE INVINCIBLES
TEAM TWO
Bucked
Irished
Sainted
Hammered
Ripped

THE UNSTOPPABLES
TEAM ONE
Furied
Merried

COWBOYS OF
CRESTED BUTTE
A Cowboy Falls
A Cowboy's Dance
A Cowboy's Kiss
A Cowboy Stays
A Cowboy Wins

Table of Contents

Prologue

I took a deep breath, making sure there were no holes in the story I was about to tell. I had to sell it and sell it good because the people I was lying to were trained to recognize even the most minute mistruths.

If I failed to convince any one of them, the house of cards I'd carefully built would come tumbling down.

"You better be fucking sure you can protect me, Cope," the agent I'd handled since the beginning of both our careers said last night when I told him his arrest was scheduled for this morning.

"You've trusted me this far, don't blow it now by panicking."

"I'll be the one locked up in a cell like a goddamn sitting duck."

"Just keep your mouth shut and let me handle it like I always do. If you don't, every risk we've taken in the last seven years will be for nothing." I didn't need to add that if he talked, I'd fucking kill him.

1

Ali

"The view from here is spectacular," said the doorman who delivered my bags to the luxurious corner loft that would be mine to live in, rent-free, for the next six months. "You can see all the way to the United States Capitol."

"I'll take your word for it," I muttered, refusing to look to the floor-to-ceiling windows where he stood. The apartment, with its high ceilings, exposed brick, and gourmet kitchen, was the nicest I'd ever seen, let alone lived in.

"Want your bags in here?" he asked.

"Sure." I followed him into one of the two bedrooms and saw it had an en suite bath to die for, with a huge jetted tub plus a shower I could hold a party in—once I knew anyone in DC.

"Is there anything else I can assist with?"

"Not for now, thanks." I took the twenty I'd set aside out of my pocket and handed it to him.

"Press one if you change your mind," he said, pointing to an intercom just inside the front door. "Oh, and if you're hungry, there's a café in the building across the street that has great food."

Once he was gone, I took off my jacket, threw it on one of the chairs in the open-concept space, pulled my laptop out of my bag, and set it on the kitchen bar.

I stretched my muscles, achy from a day of travel, and looked longingly at the high-end stationary bike sitting within a foot of the windows. Sadly, my debilitating fear of heights would prevent me from venturing too close.

When the doorman mentioned the café, I realized I hadn't eaten all day. If I didn't soon, I wouldn't be able to concentrate enough to get the work done that I needed to tonight.

I left my swanky apartment and got into the waiting elevator. With my acrophobia, taking it down was terrifying, but I didn't have the energy to walk down thirty flights of stairs, no matter how much I needed the exercise.

I pressed the button for the lobby, held on tightly to the side rail, and closed my eyes. The sinking feeling in my stomach made me consider that maybe I wasn't as hungry as I thought.

By the time I walked from the bank of elevators and out the front door, my hunger pains had returned. I opened the door to the café and approached the counter at the same time a man came in through another entrance.

He was staring at his phone and didn't notice I was there before him. He looked up at the menu board.

"I'll have a gyro salad. Thanks, Lindsey."

"We're running behind. It'll be about ten minutes, if that's okay."

I cleared my throat, which he didn't notice, in the same way he paid no attention to the woman behind the counter.

If I weren't angry-hungry, I would've let the whole thing go, but I was, and that, combined with the café running behind, pissed me the hell off. "Excuse me, but I was here first."

No response. In fact, no reaction. He turned his back and leaned against the display case, something I was sure the employees who had to clean it didn't appreciate.

I said it again, only louder.

When the man—the very handsome man with dark brown hair and eyes I could see were green—turned around and looked straight at me, I nearly gasped. Standing less than a foot from me was Sumner Copeland, whose photos I'd studied, and yet I hadn't recognized him when he first walked in.

"What did you say?"

"I…um…said I was here first."

He shrugged and went back to his phone.

"He gets lost in his own world," said the woman he'd called Lindsey. "What can I get you?"

I couldn't think straight; I couldn't even focus on the menu. If I weren't starving, I'd walk out. "I'll have the gyro salad also."

"Anything else?" she asked, punching my order into the computer.

"Hey, Linds, we're all out of gyro. That last order was it for today."

I hadn't formed my own opinion about Sumner Copeland—until now. *The muscle-bound jerk was an asshole.*

"What was that? Did you just call me an asshole?"

Had I said it out loud? I looked at Lindsey, who was trying not to laugh, so I must have. I wasn't going to lie, and I sure as hell wasn't going to apologize. "Yep. I sure did."

He put his phone in his pocket. "Why?"

"First, I was here before you. Second, I wanted the gyro salad, which I could've had if you hadn't butted in front of me and taken the last order."

He pointed up at the menu. "They have lots of other things. The cobb salad is good."

"I don't want a cobb salad."

"Let her have the gyro," I heard Lindsey say.

"What? No! That's ridiculous."

"Tell you what," she offered. "Order anything you want. It'll be on the house, and if you come back tomorrow, I'll save you some gyro."

"That's very nice of you, but this isn't your fault," I said, glaring up at the man next to me. How the hell tall was he? His dossier said six-something. His muscular chest looked to be at least three feet wide. I couldn't help but continue my perusal down his body. The sleeves of his collared shirt were tight around his chiseled arms, and the pair of faded jeans he wore hugged his thighs.

"The menu is up there," he said, pointing.

"What?"

He pointed again at the board and then at Lindsey. "You're keeping her waiting."

"You know what? Forget it. I lost my appetite." I walked toward the same door I came in, but stopped and thanked the woman behind the counter. "I'll come back another time."

She smiled and waved. "Have a good one, girl."

2

Cope

"Cope," said Lindsey in a tone of voice that sounded like my mother. "That wasn't nice."

I watched the little spitfire use the crosswalk and go inside the building across the way. Her brown hair was pulled up in a ponytail that swayed in time with her ass as she walked.

She had on clothes that looked more like she should be working out—I hated it when women wore yoga pants and training tanks as everyday clothing—but the ensemble accentuated her fit body in a way that it wouldn't have flattered one less athletic.

Even though she was mad as hell—over a salad, who does that—she was gorgeous. I could only imagine how pretty she'd be if she smiled, not something I'd likely ever see since I doubted I'd run into her again in a city with a population closing in on a million.

Thirty-five years ago, when my father, the senior Senator from the State of Louisiana, with a record of being the second-most conservative member of congress, arrived in the district, the population was half what it was now.

I was still waiting on my salad when I saw her come back out of the building a few minutes later, this time, dressed in a pair of jeans and a blouse. She walked in the opposite direction, toward the pub down the way. The food wasn't as good as what they served at the café, and they certainly didn't have a gyro salad.

"Here you go," said Lindsey, looking in the same direction I was. "You should be ashamed of yourself. She was here before you."

I ate here at least once every day and didn't want to piss off the woman who almost always took my order. "Tell you what, the next time she comes in, I'll pay for her order."

My phone chimed with a message from my mother, and I groaned. What was wrong with me? How in the hell had I forgotten that today was Sunday and I was having dinner with my parents? I walked out, leaving the to-go container sitting on the counter.

"You're late, Sumner," my mother said when I walked into the kitchen and kissed her cheek.

"Is he here?"

"They're in your father's study."

"Ah, there he is," said my father, motioning me closer. "Ed, this is my son, Sumner. Son, you know Director Fisk."

"Sumner, it's a pleasure. I've heard a lot about you."

"From my father, no doubt." I shook the hand of the man who was three rungs above my boss, and hoped that asking my father to arrange a meeting between me and the new director of the CIA wouldn't blow up in my face.

"Actually, no. I understand you were the person who took down Irish Warrick."

"There was a team, sir."

My father clapped me on the back. "What did I tell you, Ed?"

"Dad…"

"Look," said Fisk. "They call you Cope, right?"

"Yes, sir."

"The trial gets underway tomorrow. I'm assuming that's why you asked for this meeting."

My father cleared his throat. "If you gentlemen will excuse me, I'll see how dinner is coming along." He left the room, closing the door behind him.

I took a deep breath, knowing that what I was about to do could end my career, but worse, if it didn't work, it could cost the lives of CIA agents around the world.

After dinner, I walked the director to his car. When I came back, my father was waiting on the porch. "Dad, I—"

"Come with me," he said, leading me back into his study. "Have a seat, and tell me what the hell that was all about."

My father was the sitting chair of the United States Senate Select Committee on Intelligence, the whole reason he'd been able to get me an audience with Fisk.

"I can't talk to you about this, Dad."

He sat down in the chair behind his desk, turned, and looked out the window.

3

Ali

I tossed the container that held the rest of my half-eaten burger into the trash, not even sure why I'd brought it back to the apartment.

I pulled my cell phone out of my bag when I heard it ringing.

"Hey, Jessica. I was just getting ready to call you."

"Are you settled?" asked my boss as of yesterday.

"This apartment is incredible."

"More importantly, ideally located."

"Right."

"You ready for tomorrow?"

"I'm about to take another look at my notes."

"Give me a call when it wraps up, and try to get some rest."

The alarm on the bedside table went off at five, jarring me awake. I was still on West Coast time, which meant, for me, it was two. I got up and padded my way into the kitchen, wishing I'd figured out how to use the coffee maker before I went to sleep. It was far too complicated this early in the morning.

I walked as close to the windows as I could get without having a panic attack and stood on my tiptoes to see if the café across the way was open. Lights were on; that was promising.

Before I could make up my mind whether to get dressed and go down to grab a cup of coffee—which would entail taking the elevator—or attempt to figure out the machine that looked like it would take a barista's degree to use, a light in the apartment directly across from mine came on.

It had the same floor-to-ceiling windows and an exercise bike sitting in the same location as the one in this apartment. Although *bike* was too simplistic to describe this thing. Like the coffeemaker, operating it would take a degree in fitness training.

When I saw someone walking toward it, I jumped back. *Oh my God.* It was Sumner Copeland. He was shirtless—and hot as fuck.

I rested against the exposed brick wall, wishing I could take another peek, but knowing I couldn't risk him seeing me. Since I couldn't stare at him, I went back to the kitchen and stared longingly at the coffee machine. It would be easier, and hopefully quicker, to tackle it than to go across the street to buy a cup, so I searched up an instruction video. Fifteen minutes later, I was rewarded with the best coffee I'd had in my life; it better be, since according to the website, the thing cost thousands.

The elevator ride to the parking garage didn't make me as queasy as it had the day before; there was a chance I'd be used to it within a few days. After all, I had figured out how to use the fancy coffee machine. As my mother always said, I could do anything I set my mind to, I just had to want it badly enough. Who knew? Maybe tomorrow I'd overcome my fear of heights enough to check out the exercise bike.

I looked at my reflection in the polished glass of the elevator, trying to determine if I'd gone overboard in my decision to wear a conservative suit, or if I should've gone more casual. I shrugged. Too late to change my mind now.

My older-model car looked pathetic in my desig-nated spot between two BMWs, but this morning, I was thankful the apartment came with a paid space. It would be insanely expensive to keep a car in DC otherwise, and right now, I needed it.

It would be at least an hour to get to the United States Eastern District Court of Virginia, longer if traffic was bad. Taking a car service would've probably cost more than the coffee maker, and by the time I figured out how to get there via public transportation, the opening arguments in the trial I'd been assigned to cover would be over.

I arrived an hour before the scheduled court time, parked, followed the signs for security, and waited in line. Even with ten people in front of me, I should still have time to kill before the hearing began.

"Ma'am, may I see your credentials?" the man asked before I walked through the metal detector.

"Right. Sorry." I dug in my purse. "I must've left my badge in my car."

"No credentials, no entry."

"No problem," I said, but he didn't smile. "Be right back."

When I turned around, I gasped as I saw Sumner Copeland headed my way. I shielded my face and kept walking.

"Hey," I heard him say. "Aren't you the woman…"

I dropped my hand, tugged my waist-length suit jacket down, straightened my spine, and glanced beyond him to the people he'd come in with. "Yes."

"What are you doing here?"

I cocked my head, wondering how he'd react if I told him it was none of his business.

"Cope," one of the men called out, looking at his watch. "We need to get in there."

He looked over his shoulder and back at me. "Right. Okay, well…"

"Bye." I waved my fingers at him and rushed to the bank of elevators. So much for me keeping a low profile. Why did I keep running into him? And why did he have to look like a god in everything he wore—or didn't wear. I fanned myself even though it was actually kind of chilly.

Grabbing my credentials from my car, I hurried back to catch the elevator. I still had forty-five minutes, which in court time, could mean two hours, but I wanted to get a fix on people as they went in.

After going through the security line a second time, I took another elevator up to the tenth floor, found the designated courtroom, and grabbed a seat on the bench closest to the door. I took out a pen and pad, and started scribbling notes.

I was biting the end of my pen when I saw the salad-stealing, muscle-headed man of the hour walking in my direction.

I shielded my face like I had earlier, peeking through my fingers in time to see him walk into a room on the other side of the hall. I breathed a sigh of relief and went back to my notes.

"Ahem," I heard someone clear their throat less than a minute later.

I raised my head enough to see the toes of men's wingtips on the floor, pointing at me. They were close enough that if I moved my foot forward just a little, our shoes would touch.

"You didn't answer me earlier. What are you doing here?"

I had to crane my neck to see the giant's face. In fact, I had to lean back to look up at him. "How tall are you anyway, like seven feet?"

"I asked you a question."

"I'm obviously here for a…hearing."

"Which hearing?"

I closed my notebook and shoved my pen in the spiral part of it, or I tried to; it was too big to fit, so I just held it.

When I looked back up, he was studying me with his head cocked. *Oh no.* Was there something on my face? Had I gotten ink on it when I was chewing on my pen? God, I was supposed to fade into the background, but the only thing I was managing to do was call attention to myself.

He tilted his head to the other side. What was he looking at now?

"Is that a press pass?"

"Pass? No. It's a credential."

"You're with the press?" he said like it was something unpleasant on the bottom of his shoe. "Which news outlet?"

"The *Express.*"

He ran his hand through his hair and then rubbed the back of his neck. "You can't be here."

"I beg to differ, since I am."

"Come with me."

He waited, but I didn't move. "Miss…"

"Graham."

"Come with me," he repeated.

"I'm not going anywhere."

He sat on the bench, beside me. "Do you have any idea what's about to happen?"

"You're going to try to get me kicked out of the courthouse, and I already told you, I'm not leaving."

"In that courtroom," he seethed, pointing.

"Yes, I believe I do. Opening arguments in an espionage case," I snapped right back at him.

"No press allowed, so you're wasting your time."

I put my notepad and pen in my bag and folded my arms. "I've got nowhere else to be, so I think I'll continue *wasting my time* right here."

Another man stuck his head out of the door. "He's here, Cope. We're waiting for you."

"Who? Warrick?" I asked.

"Keep your voice down."

"Is it Warrick or not?"

He glared at me, which I took as a yes.

"Are you his attorney?" I asked, even though I knew better.

"No." He stood and stalked off.

No sooner was he gone than three people—two men and a woman—rushed into the courtroom. Within seconds, they were back out. One of the men banged on the door across the hallway.

It opened, but I couldn't see the person behind it. The man pushed his way in, followed by the other two. I could hear shouting right before the door closed again, but not enough to make out what they were arguing about.

Whoever man number one was, he was pissed. My hunch was that he was Warrick's attorney.

A few minutes later, I noticed another woman wearing a press credential, leaning up against the wall. I walked over and introduced myself. "Ali Graham." I reached out to shake her hand.

She looked me up and down, kind of like Chloe, my best friend from home, did whenever she met someone new. She said it made her feel like she had the upper hand. It was too late for me to do the same thing, so I asked, "Who are you?"

She laughed and shook my outstretched hand. "I'm TJ, with AP."

"With AP?"

"Freelance, but they place most everything I write."

Wait. "Are you *TJ Hunter*?" The woman had won every journalistic award ever given.

We both turned our heads when a door opened. The three people I'd seen go in last, came out with a fourth.

"There he is," murmured TJ.

I would've known even if she hadn't said anything. I'd seen plenty of photos of Paxon "Irish" Warrick.

"Scum of the fuckin' earth," she spat. "Selling out his own country—not to mention fellow agents—to China."

So much for unbiased reporting. "What about innocent until proven guilty?"

"Sumner Copeland put an airtight case together, I can assure you of that."

"Sumner Copeland? Is he the prosecutor?" I asked, even though I already knew exactly who he was.

TJ laughed. "No, sweetheart. He was Warrick's handler."

"At the CIA?"

"Yep."

When the door opened again, the man himself walked out.

"Hey, Stella. How are you?" He walked over and hugged TJ.

"Cope, have you met Ali Graham?"

"I have. We had a little mix-up over a salad yester-day." He leaned forward and kissed the other woman's cheek. "I gotta get in there. See you later, Stell." He walked away but looked over his shoulder. "You too, Tally."

"It's Ali."

TJ laughed. "He knows it is."

"Then, why'd he call me Tally?"

"Look it up, sis. Tally Graham."

"Why does he call you Stella?" I rolled my eyes when it dawned on me that Stella Hunter had been a famous actress. "Never mind."

"I knew you were smart. She was my grandmother. What's the deal with the salad?"

"It isn't that interesting."

"Honey, we're going to be sitting out here for at least three hours. Plain lettuce is going to be interesting."

"How do you know him?" I asked an hour later.

"Press conferences. You know who his father is, right?"

"Remind me."

"Senator Henry Clay Copeland?"

"Chair of the United States Senate Select Committee on Intelligence?"

"That's right, sis."

"Will he give you a story?"

"Cope?"

I nodded.

"No fuckin' way in hell," she muttered under her breath.

The courtroom door swung open, and Cope stalked out ahead of everyone else.

"Uh-oh," said TJ, gathering her stuff. "Come with me, kid."

"Where are we going?"

"To get the story."

4

Cope

I was ready to throttle Irish. Did he really need me to hold his fucking hand through this whole thing? He was wasting valuable time, and I needed him to knock it off.

I damn near looked behind me when I walked out of the courtroom, to see if Ali was still in the hallway with Stella. I couldn't explain why she was on my mind when it was crowded with a thousand other things. Important things. Like whether or not I could salvage my career or if I'd end up in jail like Irish was.

I stepped onto the elevator and was waiting for the doors to close when I saw the little spitfire walk past with Stella. I leaned against the back panel and closed my eyes.

"Who was the hot number with Stella?" questioned the attorney I'd asked to fly in from Texas, Sterling Anderson, aka Hammer.

"A reporter with the *Express.*"

"Oh. Well, *shit.* That's disappointing."

Tell me about it. Her being a reporter meant I had to stay away from her, not just now, but forever. Between my job and the fact that my father was a senator, the last person I could afford to have any kind of association with was someone with the press.

But, damn, I wanted to associate all over her. She was so beautiful, big blue eyes, and that tight little body—*fuck*. I worked out hard every day, but it wouldn't surprise me if Lois Lane had a lower percentage of body fat than I did.

Apart from her looks, I loved how she pushed right back at me, got in my face about the stupid salad that I never ate anyway. Whenever I thought about it, I felt like an asshole.

And earlier today, when I told her she couldn't be in the courthouse, she didn't back down. There was something about her that said she never would.

"See ya tomorrow," Hammer said as he exited the elevator a floor above where I'd parked.

I was thinking through everything I still had to do that afternoon as I stepped off on my floor. Something—someone—to my right caught my eye. The reporter. It looked like there was something up with her car.

"Need help?" I asked before I realized she was on the phone. Her eyes met mine, and she held up a finger. Not *that* finger, even though I might've deserved it, given how I'd treated her since we met.

"I'm on hold with roadside assistance," she told me.

"What's the problem?"

"It won't start. Probably the battery."

"I'll pull my car around and give it a jump."

"That's okay. I'm sure they'll be here—" She put her finger in her ear to block out the noise of the cars leaving the structure. "I'm sorry, what did you say? It sounded like you said it would be three hours." She rested against her car and then looked down at her white blouse that was now dirty. "Oh, you did say three hours? Well, okay." She hit disconnect on her phone and looked over at me. "I guess things are a lot busier around here than they are in Sunnyville."

"Sunnyville?"

"Where I'm from. It's a small town in California."

"Right. Okay, well, let me see if I can get it started."

"Thanks…" Her voice trailed off while she studied something on her phone.

"Everything okay?"

She opened her mouth like she was going to respond and then snapped it closed. The smile she gave me was freakishly fake. "Everything is fine."

I walked to my car, took off my jacket, and hung it in the back seat. Before I started it up, I checked the news feeds to see if there was something going on that had caused her reaction. The first headline jumped out at me.

CIA to Make Deal with China Spy

What the fuck? Who in the hell? I checked the byline. *Associated fucking Press.* I scrolled through my contacts and hit the button to call Stella.

"Cope, I was just—"

"Save it. You wanna tell me where you get off, reporting anything about this trial, let alone that there's a deal in the works? Who's your source, Stella?"

"Whoa, you better back way the fuck up, Cope. You're jumping to too many conclusions for me to even continue this conversation."

"AP byline, Stella. I saw you and one other reporter at the courthouse today."

"Like I said, Cope, fuck of a lot of assumptions."

When she ended the call, I threw my phone on the seat, ready to peel out of the parking lot. Fortunately, I remembered Ali and her dead battery before I did. Forgetting her would've only confirmed I was the asshole she already believed I was.

"You saw it," she said when I got out after pulling my car beside hers.

"Yeah, I saw it." I expected her to defend Stella, but she didn't.

"I really appreciate this," she said instead when I dug my jumper cables out of my trunk.

After three tries, I knew Ali's battery was beyond a jump start. I had to get to the office and do damage control on the AP report, but I didn't feel comfortable leaving her here alone.

"Look, come with me. I have a few things to take care of, and then I can drop you at your building."

"But…my car."

"Right. Let me put out some fires, and then we'll go get you a new battery."

"You don't have to do that, Mr. Cope. I know you're very busy."

"It's Cope, and it's the least I can do after…"

"What?"

"I was a pretty major jackass about the salad."

"I could've ordered something else. I was just past the point of no return."

"Hangry?"

"Exactly." She laughed. It was a beautiful sound. "So about the report…"

"Ali…right?"

She nodded.

"I'm happy to help you with your car, but as far as anything to do with the trial, I can't talk about it. Especially to you."

She turned her head so I couldn't see her face. "Got it."

It took two hours to get from the district court to the agency headquarters in Langley, and neither of us said another word. Once again, I felt like a dick for snapping at her, but she had to understand that even though she was in the car with me, it would've been better if we didn't even know each other's names.

I pulled into the underground parking. "I'll try to be quick."

"You really don't have to do this."

"I'm doing it, okay?" I got half a smile, and that was good enough for me.

"There are some public galleries you can roam around in," I told her when the elevator stopped at the main lobby. "Just give me a few minutes, and then we'll take care of your car."

I left her in the lobby and took the elevator six floors up. The instant I got off, I knew shit had hit the fan. I didn't even make it to my office before my boss, Kellen "Money" McTiernan, motioned me into his and slammed the door behind me. "What the fuck, Cope?"

There was nothing he or I could say that would change the present optics. "I'm as angry as you are, sir."

I inwardly groaned when the team on the Warrick sting filed in one by one, followed by two people from the Office of Public Affairs. The last thing I needed was ten more people sticking their noses into this.

The bullshit response to the leak that would've taken me thirty minutes to craft if I were left alone—and that would've been with revisions—took the people in the room over two hours to do, and they still weren't finished arguing about it.

I leaned back in my chair and looked at my watch, knowing I was forgetting something.

Ali.

"Shit!"

Every head in the room turned and looked at me when I stood and collected the crap I had spread out on the table. "There's something I need to take care of."

"Cope?" said McTiernan.

I motioned with my head for him to follow me out to the hall. Thankfully, he did.

"I mean no disrespect, sir."

"Money."

"Okay. Money. But the last two hours have been…" I scrubbed my face with my hand, wishing I had thought through what I was going to say.

"A Charlie Foxtrot." He finished my sentence for me. "I see that now. It's the 'cooks in the kitchen' thing."

"I have something I have to do, but I can come back."

"Don't bother. You've got a long few days ahead of you. Go home. Figure out who the hell was there today that could've seen something, heard something, guessed something, and then tomorrow, if they're back, toss 'em out on their ass."

"Copy that, sir…I mean, Money."

"Sorry for the overreaction, Cope." He clapped me on the back, and I shook my head.

"This thing with Irish has had us all spun up for months."

After he told me to check in with him the next day, I raced to my office, grabbed everything I thought I might need, shoved it into my messenger bag, and rushed out. When I saw another handler, an incessant talker, waiting for the elevator. I spun around and took the stairs all the way down to the lobby.

I burst through the door and stopped in my tracks. I didn't see her. Was she still wandering around?

"Hey, Cope." Bernie, the security guard I'd seen at the desk earlier when I left Ali in the lobby, motioned me over. "She asked me to give you this." It was a folded piece of paper.

"How long ago did she leave?"

"Not too long."

I looked up at the ceiling and groaned. I couldn't do anything right where this woman was concerned. I walked back in the direction of the elevator, hit the button, and opened the note.

Thanks for the lift back. I owe you one.

One what? A giant fuck you?

5

Ali

As far as days went, this one was expensive. I forgot to call the roadside service company to tell them I was leaving, so they charged me a hundred bucks for what they said was a "no show."

When I finally got back to my car—via the car service, which also cost over a hundred dollars—and called roadside assistance a second time, they agreed my battery was dead, but not that I needed a new one. Instead, they predicted there was an issue with my electrical system.

I talked to the security people in the parking garage and asked if I could leave my car there overnight until I figured out what to do with it. They said I could, but there was a hundred-dollar fee for that too.

Roadside service towed my car to a service station within the free five-mile radius, which meant I had to take the car service back to my apartment. If I added in what it would cost me to get back for the hearing the next day, plus getting my car fixed, I figured I was looking at a thousand dollars easy.

None of this was Sumner Copeland's fault, except I'd wasted so much time sitting in the stupid CIA building, waiting for him. I should've left as soon as we got there. Then I should've left when an hour passed and he still hadn't come down. When it hit the two-hour mark, I was furious. Not to mention that every time the elevator door opened, I worried someone who knew me would get off.

My guess was Cope had forgotten all about me. I mean, would it have been so hard to send some intern down to tell me it was going to take a lot longer than he'd expected?

The driver pulled up to my building, and I crawled out of the back seat, dead tired and laden with my messenger bag, my gym bag, and some other stuff from my car that I'd thrown into a paper bag. I was about to walk into my building when I heard someone shouting.

"Miss, miss, wait!" I turned around and saw Lindsey from the café running toward me, carrying yet another bag.

"Can I help you?" I asked.

"This is from…damn, I'm out of shape." She tried to catch her breath. "Anyway, this is from Cope. You just missed him." She took another deep breath. "He was waiting to give it to you himself, but then he got a call."

"Look, Lindsey, right?"

She nodded, still trying to catch her breath.

"This is really sweet, but I've had a really long, really hard day, and I don't have much of an appetite."

"He told me. At least his part in it. I'll tell you, he really feels awful about it. Just take this. It's dinner, plus stuff for breakfast and lunch tomorrow. By the looks of you, it'll probably last you all week."

"By the looks of me?" I asked, not bothering to hide my scowl.

"You're tiny. You probably don't eat more than a bite or two at every meal, am I right?"

I was dead tired, my feet were killing me, I was starving even though I'd lied and said I wasn't, and I was irritable. Nothing I was going through was the fault of the woman who'd run across the street to give me food.

I smiled and shook my head. "You'd be surprised how much I can pack away. My grandma always said

I had the appetite of an offensive lineman. Thank you for this. I really do appreciate it."

"There's silverware in there and napkins, plus instructions for heating it all up. Oh, and there's dessert too. I'm sorry you had such a shitty day." She tried to hand me the bag, but with everything I was carrying, I had no way to take it.

"You want me to bring this upstairs for you?"

"No, thanks. I'll get it."

I looked up when I saw the man who'd left me sitting in the lobby of a building for two hours, about to cross the street. "I gotta go. Thanks again." I stuck out one finger, and she hung the bag on it.

"You sure you don't want help?"

"Nope, I got it. Thanks," I said, hoping my finger wouldn't bend back any farther before I got upstairs.

I rushed in the revolving door and over to the elevator, willing one of them to open when I hit the call button with my elbow.

"Ali," I heard Cope call out, but pretended I didn't. Not that it mattered, because the damn elevators seemed to all be stuck on the tenth floor. Where the hell was the doorman, anyway?

"Ali, I'm glad I caught you."

I wasn't. I heard a ding and the sound of doors opening.

"I'm sorry about earlier. Things really hit the fan, and it took a lot longer—"

"Tell the truth," I said, stepping into my escape route. "You forgot all about me." I set the bag of food down on the floor and rummaged around for my key card, only remembering I needed it when the elevator didn't move. In that time, he'd stepped inside.

"You're right. I did forget."

I found the card and looked up at him. "Okay. Well, thanks for the food."

"Can I ride up with you? Help you with that?"

"No, I got it."

Someone else rushed into the elevator and stuck his card in the slot. "What floor?" he said, looking first at me and then at Cope.

"Thirtieth."

The man hit the button for twenty-four and then the one for thirty. I didn't speak again until he got out.

"How did you know my floor?" I said as soon as the doors closed. They opened again, and he still hadn't answered me.

"Well?"

"I'll explain when we're inside."

"Inside? You're not coming inside." I did my damnedest to pick up the bag of food while juggling the rest of my crap.

"Quit being so stubborn and let me help you."

Cope grabbed the food and then took my messenger bag off my shoulder. He motioned toward my door, because he knew which one it was. That alone was enough to give me a panic attack.

I stuck the key card into the slot in the door, and when it clicked, Cope grasped the knob and held it open for me. I stepped over the threshold, dropped the bags I was still carrying, and held out my hands for the two he had.

"Thanks for your help."

He shook his head, turned his body sideways, and walked past me and into the kitchen.

"Hey! I didn't invite you in." The heavy door slammed behind me as I stalked after him.

He set the bags on the kitchen counter, and instead of walking back out, he sauntered toward the windows.

"Come here," he said, motioning to me.

"What?"

"Come here," he repeated, waving his arm. I walked as far as I comfortably could.

"Here," he said again, pointing.

"Just tell me."

"I'm not going to tell you; I'm going to show you how I know."

"You can show me from here."

"God, are you seriously this stubborn?" He stalked back to me and tried to take my hand, but I stuck it behind my back. He studied me for a few seconds. "You can't walk over to the windows, can you?"

"I can. I don't want to."

"Take another step forward."

An imaginary line went from the wall, over to the far end of the dining room table. I already knew I couldn't walk beyond it without getting vertigo. I spun around and stomped back to the kitchen. I was almost to the counter when I felt an arm snake around my waist.

"What are you doing?" I shrieked when he lifted me from the floor and carried me over to the windows. He was beyond my line, and I still hadn't been able to wriggle out of his grasp. "Please don't," I begged him, tears threatening.

He set me down between him and the window but didn't take his arm from around my waist. "I'm right there," he said in a soft voice as he pointed at the apartment I already knew he lived in. "And you're okay. Your feet are on the floor, and you aren't going to fall."

"I don't like heights," I muttered.

"Figured that." He turned to the left and spun me along with him. "Too bad because, look at that view."

In the distance, I saw the United States Capitol Building, just like the doorman had said. It truly was breathtaking.

"I can tell you, that view never gets old." His mouth was still close to my ear, and I could feel his breath on my neck.

"You can let go now."

"Can I? You sure?"

When he started to, I grabbed his arm and kept it where it was. "Maybe just walk me back."

He turned again, so I was facing the kitchen.

"I'm good now."

He dropped his arm from around my waist, but I could feel his fingers on the small of my back.

"I have one of those," he said, pointing to the exer-cise bike. "Been on it?"

I took a container out of the bag, set it on the counter, and tilted my head. "Look where it is."

"Yeah?"

"No, I haven't been on it. If I had, it wouldn't still be sitting *there*." I did want to try it out, though, and could use the exercise. Maybe over the weekend, I'd ask one of the doormen to help me move it away from the windows.

I watched Cope walk over, kneel down, and flip a switch. "Have you ever tried out one of these? They're amazing." He tapped his finger on the screen. "The software needs to update, but once it does, I can show you one of its really cool features."

I had the containers out of the bag and stuck my fork into what looked like a gyro salad. "Oh my God," I groaned when I took a bite of the succulent meat. "This is so good." I took two more bites, barely swallowing in between. "No wonder you wouldn't give it up."

He walked over and stood across the counter from me. "I'm sorry about that too."

"Too?"

"And I'm sorry about forgetting you were waiting in the lobby for me today."

"And?"

He cocked his head.

"What else are you sorry for?"

His eyes opened wide. He looked at the containers in front of me, and then he shrugged. "There's more?"

"Telling me I couldn't be at the courthouse, for starters."

"I'm not sure I owe you an apology for that."

"You were rude." I took two more bites, closing my eyes as I chewed, moaning at how good it tasted.

"Anything else?"

My mouth was full, so I nodded.

"What?" he asked right before I stabbed another piece of the meat.

"You snapped at me in the car."

He rolled his eyes. "No, I didn't."

"'As far as anything to do with the trial, I can't talk about it. Especially to you.'"

"I was stating a fact. I didn't snap."

I pushed aside the lettuce, looking for another piece of the meat, smiling when I found one.

He reached over and opened one of the containers. Inside was baklava, and when he took a piece, I smacked the back of his hand with my fork. "Ouch! Why'd you do that?"

"Put it back."

He didn't. He took a bite, and I glared at him.

"That was mine."

"I bought it."

"Oh, is that how it works? Indian giver much?"

"*Indian giver?* You better watch it, Miss Graham. Word gets out you made an ethnic slur in the nation's capital, you might get your hand slapped. Maybe by a fork." He rubbed where I'd hit him.

When I opened another container and, in it, found quiche, Cope snapped up another piece of baklava.

"There should be soup and rolls in one of the smaller bags."

I grabbed the container of the sweet Greek dessert and moved it out of his reach.

"Greedy," he muttered, licking his fingers. "So, what were you going to tell me about the report?"

"What do you mean?"

"Before I snapped at you, you said, 'So about the report…'"

I was surprised he remembered, especially with how hard I was hoping he'd forget.

"Come on, Tally, give it up."

"My name is Ali."

He reached across the counter and grabbed another piece of baklava. "Tell me this: have you at least figured out who Tally is?"

"Yes, I'm not completely dense."

"Not completely?"

I punched his arm. "Not dense."

"So, who is she?"

"Tally Graham? You know I know." Tally had been the nickname of the woman who became editor-in-chief of the *Express* when her husband, who previously held the job, suffered a debilitating stroke. Few outside the industry knew the story, though.

"All right. Good enough. Now tell me what you know about the report."

"I didn't say I knew anything."

"You were going to."

"You don't know that."

"Did you see something suspicious?"

"I don't know what you're talking about."

"Not something, but someone?"

Fuck, he was good. With everything that happened, I'd forgotten all about the man I saw when I walked from the elevator to my car. I didn't realize it at the time, but the car the guy had been standing near was Cope's. Not that I thought he'd had anything to do with the report. I'd credited Stella with the false leak.

"Could you pick him out of a lineup?"

"I didn't say I saw anyone." I stood and tossed the empty food containers in the trash bin, hoping he'd drop it.

"Was he hot or something?"

I spun around. "Was who hot?"

"You just got flustered. What happened? Did whoever you saw push all your buttons, Tally?"

"Don't call me that."

"It's a compliment, you know."

"Whatever."

"Come on, just tell me."

"All right. I did see someone in the garage, but I don't think he had anything to do with the report of a deal."

"What made you notice him?"

"He gave me the creeps."

"Where was he when he creeped on you?"

"He didn't do anything *on* me. He was in the garage, near your car, actually. Although at the time, I didn't know it was yours."

"What did he look like?"

"Asian."

Cope shook his head. "Now I understand. You thought I was going to call you out on it."

"No…" God, why was I lying about it? "Yes."

"It's okay. You have to describe him somehow. What else do you remember about him?"

I shook my head. "Nothing." My mind was reeling, wondering how he'd managed to get me to tell him about the guy.

"It's okay. There are security cameras. We'll take a look when we're at the courthouse tomorrow."

"You will. I won't."

"What does that mean?"

"I have to figure out what to do about my car."

"Done."

"What's done?" I smacked his hand when he started to take another piece of baklava.

"Ouch." He shook his hand. "I'll get you more."

"Tonight?"

"Do you want to hear what I did about your car?"

I folded my arms. When he stood and turned his back, I took the last two pieces of the sweet, sticky, Greek dessert. He spun around, looked at the empty container, and then at me.

"So…what did you do?"

"I bought a battery. We'll switch it out with the old one, and you'll be good to go."

I shook my head. "It isn't that simple. I had it towed. The roadside guy said it was probably my electrical system."

"It isn't."

"What are you, a car guru?"

"No, what I am is a guy—"

"You can't be serious."

"Let me finish. I'm a guy who works for the CIA, which means I see dishonesty on a daily basis. I'd be willing to bet that the 'roadside guy' has an in with the mechanic where he took your car. They'll tell you it's something way worse than a seventy-dollar battery and then split the proceeds of your outlandish bill."

"They wouldn't do that."

Cope shook his head. "Of course they would."

"You're wrong."

"Wanna bet?"

"Sure. What? Another order of baklava?"

"Nope. I'm thinking it's gotta be more important than that."

I studied him. He was serious about this. "Why?"

"I don't know."

6

Cope

"What do you mean you don't know?" she asked.

I couldn't explain it, but there was something about this woman. "If I'm right, you'll try out the bike. And you won't move it."

"What? That's crazy. No. And I didn't say I wanted to bet. I just want to get my car fixed so I can do my job."

"You said 'sure.'"

Ali put her hands on her hips. "You're a twelve-year-old in a grown man's body. I may have said sure, but I didn't shake on it, so no bet."

"If I lose, I'll give you a story." *What the fuck?* Had those words just come out of my mouth? I'll give her a story? Had I lost my mind?

"Which story?"

"I don't know. A good one."

She shook her head. "Warrick's story." Before I could say anything, she held up her hand. "Warrick's trial. An exclusive. Daily updates."

I was ninety-nine percent certain I was right about the mechanic scamming her, but if I wasn't, there was no way I could give her what she was asking for.

"That's what I thought." Ali began putting lids on the food containers and loading them into the fridge.

"Not really a fair bet."

She set the last container back on the counter and rested her hands on either side of it. "I've had a really long and not-so-great day. I'm tired, and I have to get up really early tomorrow to figure out how in the hell I'm going to get all the way down to Virginia without it costing me a fortune. So, if you wouldn't mind…"

"I told you I'd give you a ride."

"I don't think that's a good idea."

"I won't forget about you again, if that's what you're worried about. I'll stop in the garage before I go up to my apartment, and put the battery on my seat." I saw the hint of a smile.

"That's how memorable I am? The only way you won't forget about me is if you almost sit on a big black box?"

"It would just be a precaution." When she shrugged, I knew I had her. "I'll even get coffee for the road."

"What else?"

"For the road?"

She nodded.

"Um…" I'd already delivered the gyro salad; that wouldn't be good in the morning, anyway. "Yogurt with granola and fruit."

"Okay."

"Okay, you'll ride with me tomorrow?"

She covered her mouth with her hand, yawned, and nodded.

"Goodnight, Ali," I said, walking over and standing right in front of her. "We'll leave at six. That will give me time to look at your car before I have to be at the courthouse."

"You don't have to do this."

"I want to." She looked dead-on-her-feet tired and so fucking beautiful I wanted to pick her up, carry her into the bedroom, and…tuck her in.

"Stop looking at me like that."

I smiled. "Like what?"

"You know." Ali took a step to the side and walked around me. "Goodnight, Cope."

I got on the elevator, feeling like I'd just won some kind of prize. Why did I feel so elated when I was the one doing her a favor?

The next morning, when I got in the car after Ali did, I wished I hadn't brought coffee. She smelled so damn good when she stood next to me while I unlocked the passenger door and opened it for her. It wasn't perfume; it was just her. The smell of coffee, though, overpowered the smell of her. I smiled and rolled my eyes, remembering the conversation we'd had the night before.

"Last chance if you want to change your mind about our bet."

"No, thanks."

I pointed to the two stainless steel travel mugs of coffee sitting in the holders. "One's black, one has cream and sugar."

"Which one is yours?"

"Whichever one you don't want."

She picked up the one closest to her, opened the lid, closed it, and took a sip.

"Black, huh?"

"I don't like sugar in my coffee."

"Noted."

She turned her head away and looked out the window. "I doubt it's knowledge you'll need in the future."

"There's food in a bag on the back seat," I said as I pulled out of the garage and onto the street. This early in the morning, it would only take us a little over an hour to get to the area where the garage and courthouse were. My guess was it would take me thirty minutes to switch out her battery. The courthouse didn't open until nine, so we might have time to kill.

"Everything okay?" I asked when we'd been on the road for a half hour and she hadn't said anything.

"It's nice to be able to look at the scenery. This is a prettier drive than the one back yesterday."

"This is my favorite way to go when I have time."

"Do you have to drive to the courthouse often?"

"Not the courthouse, but the area."

"What's there?"

"Lots of cool things."

She turned and looked at me for the first time since we left the parking garage. "Like what?"

"A few museums, stuff like that."

"What museums?"

"One is a Civil War museum."

"That does sound cool."

It was one of my favorite places. My grandfather used to take me there when I was a kid. Now, when the stress of my job got to be too much, I'd jump in the car and drive down there. Just sitting on a bench and people watching, like my gramps and I used to, was enough to melt my tension away.

"I'd like to see it sometime. It sounds interesting."

"Yeah?"

"There's nothing like that in California." She laughed. "Lots of Spanish missions, though."

"I'd like to see a mission sometime."

"Yeah?" she asked like I had.

We spent the rest of the drive talking about the places where we grew up. They couldn't have been more different.

The mechanic wasn't open when we got there, but we only had about fifteen minutes to wait.

"I shouldn't have drank so much coffee," I heard her mumble.

I started the car back up and drove down the road to a diner I knew was open. "I need to use the facilities too," I explained when I parked near the front door.

I waited for her by the entrance after I'd used the men's room.

"Hang on," she said, holding up a finger when I opened the door to go out.

"I was wondering if I could get a piece of that pie to go," she said to the waitress behind the counter.

"Of course, darlin'. You want that warmed up?"

"No, thank you. I'm not going to eat it until later, anyway."

"Here you go, doll," said the woman. I watched Ali hand her a five-dollar bill and turn to walk away. "Miss," called out the woman, "don't forget your change."

"That's okay. Please keep it."

"I brought yogurt," I said once we were back in the car.

"I know. I just think it's rude to use the restroom and not buy anything."

"I think they're used to it."

She shrugged. "Maybe I'll be hungry later. Or you will."

There was something about her simple act of courtesy that shamed me. I doubted I'd ever be able to use a restroom again without buying something.

When we got back to the mechanic's, it was open. "Wait here. I'll be right back," I said, parking in an open space near her car.

I told the kid behind the counter why I was there and that "my girlfriend" and I had had a miscommunication the day before. She didn't realize I'd already purchased a new battery when she had the car towed.

"You want us to put that in for you?" he asked.

"I can do it, since I didn't purchase it from you."

"Have at it," he said, handing me the keys.

There were at least five things wrong with what the kid had just done, but rather than lecture him, I took care of Ali's car. The sooner we were on our way and this was behind us, the better.

As I'd predicted, after I put the new battery in, the car started up just fine. I closed the hood and walked over to her window when she rolled it down.

"Oh, no!" she gasped.

"What?"

"Your shirt!"

I looked down and saw a big black slash of grease on my crisp white dress shirt. "Not a big deal. I've got my jacket."

"I'm so sorry. Is there anything I can do?"

My imagination could conjure up all kinds of stuff Miss Ali could do for me. None of them had anything to do with my shirt...unless it involved removing it.

"I'll tell you what you can do. Climb out. I'm going to drive your car and make sure it's running okay. You can take mine."

She rolled her eyes. "I can figure out whether my car is running okay or not, Cope."

"Humor me. Consider it atoning for my ruined shirt."

She sighed, but she got out, and I handed her my keys.

"Don't forget your pie," I said, motioning to the box she'd left on the front seat after grabbing her bag.

"Actually, I got it for you since I wouldn't let you have any more baklava last night."

She was so damn cute I wanted to take her lips instead—they had to be sweeter than any dessert I'd ever tasted.

"I'll see you over there."

"Cope, wait."

"Yeah?" I said before climbing into her car.

"Thank you for doing this for me. I want you to let me reimburse you for the battery and the shirt."

I wouldn't tell her that my shirt was a gift from my mother, that it was monogrammed, or that it cost five-times what the battery did. "Tell you what, instead of reimbursing me, walk over to where that bike sits near your window and give it a go."

Her cheeks flushed. "Why is that so important to you?"

"I don't know. It just is."

When Ali shook her head and got in my car, I backed hers up and pulled out of the lot.

7

Ali

By the time I backed Cope's car out to follow him to the courthouse, the light had turned red, and I was glad. I needed a minute to remind myself who I was dealing with. I knew better than to fall for Cope's charm, but he sure as hell wasn't making it easy. He worked the handsome-enough-to-be-a-politician thing like a pro.

Add in how considerate he'd been, and before I knew it, I'd be convincing myself he wasn't such a bad guy after all. Again, I knew better.

I pulled partway out of the lot and glanced in the rearview mirror while I waited for the light to change; I needed to put on some lipstick when I got to the courthouse. I also reminded myself to make sure I had my press credentials around my neck before I went upstairs.

When I looked up to make sure the light hadn't turned green, I saw a car barreling toward me out of the corner of my eye. "Please stop," I begged out loud seconds before it slammed into the side of Cope's car.

I felt the crunch of metal as though it was inside my body. My teeth gnashed hard. I heard a sound so loud it hurt my ears milliseconds before the car's airbags deployed. They slammed into my body, both from the front and from the side.

That was the last thing I remembered.

I knew I was in a bed. I could hear lots of beeping sounds…and voices. One in particular sounded famil-iar. My eyes fluttered open, but it was too bright, so I closed them again.

My body hurt, and it was hard to breathe.

"We'll get her up to X-ray and see if anything's bro-ken," I heard another voice say. "Have you managed to reach her next of kin?"

"I'm working on it," said the familiar man's voice.

"Cope, what can I do?" I heard a woman ask.

"Get over to the courthouse. Explain there's been an accident and that I need a twenty-four-hour continuance."

"Wouldn't it be easier if you went and I stayed with her?"

"No," I heard the voice snap. It was Cope's. That's what the woman had said. "I'm not leaving her here alone."

"She won't be alone. I'll be with her." The woman's voice sounded more soothing.

"Please, Stella, just do as I ask."

I felt a hand on my arm and tried again to open my eyes. Why did the lights above me have to be so bright?

"Hey, Ali, how are you doing?" said the woman.

"Too bright," I groaned.

"Cope, she's awake. Get a nurse, and turn those lights off." I felt her squeeze my arm. "I'll let you know when you can open your eyes."

"I need you both to step outside," someone else said.

"She wants the lights off."

I heard movement.

"Go ahead and open your eyes now, sweetheart."

When I did, someone I didn't recognize was standing over me.

"What's your name, miss?"

"Um…Ali Graham," I murmured.

"Do you know what day it is, Ali?"

It hurt to talk. "Tuesday?" I whispered.

"That's right. Do you know why you're in the hospital, Ali?"

"No." I couldn't say anything else; my chest felt like a ton of bricks was sitting on it.

"You were in an accident. Do you remember any-thing about it?"

"No," I said again, wishing I didn't have to talk.

"We're going to get you up to X-ray in a few min-utes. Is there someone we can call? Do you have family who lives close by?"

I closed my eyes and shook my head but just barely. It hurt too much to try to move it more than that.

"Sir, I asked you to wait outside."

I felt fingertips brush my hair from my forehead, opened my eyes, and looked into Cope's.

"Hi, there," he murmured.

I blinked a couple of times; I was in too much pain to talk.

"I'm going to ask you a couple of questions, sweet-heart. Blink once for yes and twice for no."

"Do you mind?" the nurse growled.

"Ali, do you have family I can contact? Someone in your phone? Mom? Dad?"

I blinked twice, fast.

"Okay. Siblings?"

I repeated the movement.

"Got it. How about a contact in case of emergency?"

This time I blinked once. "Chloe," I whispered.

"Chloe. Great. Last thing, what's the password to your phone?"

"Chloe," I repeated.

"He needs the password," said the nurse.

I looked at Cope, who punched the name into my phone. "Got it. I'll give her a call, and then I'll be back."

"You can wait outside until I'm finished," said the nurse, but Cope was already gone. "Sit tight. The doctor will be in to talk to you in a few minutes."

As if I was going anywhere. Once she was gone, the reporter I'd met yesterday came in.

"You're a mess, sis," she said with a smile. "But I think Cope's a bigger one. I didn't realize you two knew each other."

"Don't," I whispered.

"You in a lot of pain?"

I slowly nodded my head.

"Well, shit, they haven't even started an IV to get you meds. I'll get on that, and then I have to get to the courthouse. Not sure anyone is going to grant a continuance because I ask, but Cope refuses to leave the hospital, so…"

I closed my eyes. I wanted to tell him he could leave, but those were too many words for me to try to string together.

"Why are you still here, Stella?" Cope said when he came back in, carrying my phone.

"I didn't want to leave Ali alone. Isn't that what you said?"

"Right. Well, I'm back."

"You go," I said with enough force that my insides seized. I squeezed my eyes shut.

"Seriously, Cope, go. I'll stay here. I want to make sure someone comes to start an IV, anyway."

I pleaded with my eyes, and he brushed my hair away from my forehead a second time. If I could talk, I'd tell him it was a losing battle. My bangs always fell forward.

"If you're sure. I won't be gone long. Just until I can get the judge to grant a continuance."

I didn't have the strength to argue or stop myself from falling to sleep. Even breathing took too much energy. I closed my eyes and let the darkness engulf me, dreaming that he leaned down and kissed my cheek.

I woke again when someone came in to start the IV. "You're going to feel a lot better really soon," a different voice said. I didn't care enough to try to open my eyes. I just hoped she was right. "Here we go," she murmured. A warm, happy feeling blanketed me, and I went back to sleep.

I had no idea how much time had passed when a man came in and introduced himself as the doctor. He asked me many of the same questions the nurse had. At some point later, I felt the bed moving. "Taking you to X-ray," a soft male voice said.

I slept off and on as they moved my body around. Whatever was in the IV definitely did its job, because I was feeling no pain.

When I opened my eyes again, I was in a room and Cope was seated in a chair next to the bed, looking at his phone.

"You're awake," he said, setting his cell down and leaning forward.

"Why are you here?"

"Nice to see you too, Ali."

I smiled. Thank God I could without feeling like my body was going to crack in two.

"To answer your question, I'm here because you were in an automobile accident this morning. Do you remember what happened?"

I closed my eyes. I remember sitting at the red light, waiting for it to change so I could pull all the way out into the intersection. After that…nothing.

"Why am I here?"

"They want to keep you for observation, given you can't remember the accident. As far as injuries, a broken arm is the worst of it."

I looked down at the cast wrapped with bright-pink fabric on my left arm.

"They'll have to see how well you heal before they decide on surgery. By the way, Chloe is on her way here."

"She is? Why?"

"You're going to need help, Ali. She also has your medical power of attorney, not that it's needed now. I strongly encourage you to appoint someone here as her second, just in case."

I closed my eyes. "I wish you hadn't asked her to come." I turned my head away.

"Hey now." He waited for me to look at him before he said anything more. "You were in a serious car accident. You aren't going to be able to function on your own once you're out of the hospital. I didn't ask Chloe to come. The minute I told her what happened, she said she'd be on the next flight out."

I turned my head away again so Cope couldn't see my tears.

"Ali," he said with a soft voice. "What's going on?"

"Your car."

Cope stood, came around to the other side of the bed, and sat in a different chair. "The last thing I care about right now is my car. Yours is running fine, by the way."

I laughed, and my eyes almost rolled back in my head. "Jesus," I groaned.

"Best not to try to expand your rib cage. That'll hurt. Your ribs aren't broken, but they are bruised."

"Bruised? I don't think so. I'm pretty sure every one of them is shattered."

"It's because of the airbags. Happens a lot to people who are as small as you are." He picked up my cell phone that was sitting on the table by the bed. "By the way, someone named Jessica has called several times."

"My boss."

"I can step out if you need to call her back."

I shook my head. "I can do it later."

"At least you didn't break your right arm."

"Why?"

"Might be hard to write."

"I'm left-handed." Although with a keyboard, I used both hands equally.

"So, are you worried about your job?"

"My job? No."

"How many assignments do you have?"

"What do you mean?"

"Besides the trial. What else?"

"That's it, so far."

When his phone vibrated, he took it out of his pocket and swiped the screen. "Chloe just landed. She'll be here as soon as she can be."

"What time is it?" I looked over at the clock, stunned to see it was almost six.

A nurse walked in and erased the name on the whiteboard and then added hers. "I'm Dolly, and before you ask, yes, that is my real name. My mama wasn't too happy with me after twenty hours of labor, I guess, so that's what she stuck me with."

She turned around and set a laptop on a rolling cart. "How are you feeling, Miss Ali?"

"Okay."

"She's wincing more often."

Dolly looked over at Cope. "Are you Miss Ali's husband? This chart says she's single." The nurse looked at me. "If he hasn't put a ring on it yet, girlfriend, you get after him about it. Don't let this one get away."

"We're just friends. Through work. Sort of," I stammered.

"In that case, you best get busy. He's a fine one. Who, I'm sorry to say…" she turned to Cope, "needs to step out for a few minutes."

"You don't have to stay," I said when he stood to leave. "I'll be fine until Chloe gets here."

He looked at me and then at the nurse before walking out.

"Damn," Dolly said once he'd left. "That man gets my blood pressure goin'."

He was hot. I'd give her that.

Dolly took my temperature and my blood pressure. "What's your pain level, Miss Ali."

"Please call me Ali, and it's a seven."

"Don't let it get above a five." She handed me what looked like a call button. "Press this whenever you feel it creeping up. It's important to stay ahead of it."

"What will happen? Will you bring me more?"

"Press it, sweet thing."

I did and nothing happened. Or maybe something did.

"You can control the delivery of your medicine yourself, to a certain extent. It'll only let you have so much. If it beeps, it means you've reached your limit. Just call me if that happens, and I'll have the doc up your dosage."

"I'm sure I'll be fine."

"I would be too if I had such a nice-lookin' man sittin' at my bedside." She patted my hand. "You need anything, hit this button." She pointed to a large box that hung on the bed rail. "You can have clear liquids tonight. We'll see about solid food in the morning."

The thought of food made my stomach turn. I'd be in no hurry for liquids or solids.

Cope came back in and sat down. Before I could say anything, he leaned forward and rested his elbows on his knees. "I've got a proposition for you."

8

Cope

Ali looked up at me with those giant blue eyes I could get lost in, and it was all I could do not to lay the world at her feet. The thing about her that made me want to do so even more, is that she wouldn't ask for it. Not ever.

"What?" she asked.

"I was thinking about our bet. You said that, if you won, I'd have to give you an exclusive about the trial. Daily updates."

"But I didn't win. You did."

"The point is, you can still write about the trial."

Her eyes scrunched. "How am I going to do that?"

"I'll give you the exclusive, your own personal daily press conference."

She tried to fold her arms in front of her but then dropped them at her sides. "Why?"

"Because you've had a string of bad luck, and I—"

"What happened to you not being able to talk about the trial, especially to me?"

"I'd be an anonymous source."

More eye scrunching.

"Stop doing that with your eyes," I told her.

"Tell me why."

"I think this could benefit us both."

She turned her head and looked in the direction of the window. It was dark, but there were plenty of lights from the city reflected in it. "I won't report anything that isn't the truth."

"I wouldn't ask you to."

"What's in it for you, Cope? You said it could benefit us both."

"If there's another false report, there would be a place to counter it."

"What do I have to do?"

"What do you mean?"

"There has to be more to it than me writing a story."

I got up, walked over to the window, and looked down at the lights of the city. I stood there long enough that I wondered if maybe Ali had gone to sleep, but when I turned around, her head was on the pillow and her eyes were open—studying me.

"Get on the bike."

She turned away, shaking her head. "Be serious."

"I am."

The door opened, and a tall brunette flew in and rushed over to the bed. "Oh my God, Al. Jesus. Can I touch you?" The woman held her hands just above Ali.

"Just be gentle," I said from my perch near the window.

"Cope, right? Give me a minute to give this girl some love, and then I'll get to you."

I smiled and watched her lean over and kiss Ali's forehead.

"You didn't need to come. I'm fine."

The woman shook her head at Ali and walked over to me, her hand outstretched. "Chloe Whitley."

"Sumner Copeland. Nice to meet you."

She looked me up and down and back up again before spinning around to face Ali.

"You told me you didn't know anyone in DC."

"I don't."

Would it make me a pussy if I admitted that hurt my feelings?

"Well, he seems to know you."

Chloe turned back around and did another once over. I was starting to feel like a piece of meat.

"If I were you, my dear Ali, I'd want to get to know this one."

"I'm sorry for all this trouble," Ali murmured. "Neither of you have to stay. Seriously, I'm fine."

"I'm actually going to take you up on that and give you two some time on your own." It was all I could do not to kiss her goodbye. "I'll see you in the morning."

"What about the trial?"

"Two-day continuance."

"Why?"

"Because of the accident."

She rolled her eyes. "This is so unnecessary."

"Like I said, I'll see you in the morning. We'll get started on that project we were talking about."

The door was almost closed behind me when I heard Ali call my name.

"What about your car?" she asked when I went back in.

I held up my keys. "Rental. Which reminds me." I handed Chloe the keys to Ali's car along with the valet ticket.

"Cope?" Ali said again when I opened the door to leave for the second time.

"Yeah?"

"Thanks for staying with me today."

I could tell myself that, like I'd told Ali, her reporting on Warrick's trial would help us both. But would it? Whether I was feeding her information or not, I wouldn't be able to control what she wrote. In the little time we'd spent together, my opinion was that Ali seemed intuitive enough to decipher the truth. I sensed that if she thought I was lying, she'd call me out on it, just like I would with her. The only difference was, she had a newspaper to do it in.

I checked the time while I waited for the elevator. Before I went home, I needed to swing by and see what I could get out of my car. It was also still early enough that I could have a conversation with Money about my plan to give the *Express* reporter an exclusive.

I'd have to spin it in such a way that he'd buy I intended it as a response to the leak from yesterday— rather than me helping a woman I found so attractive that she was becoming all I thought about.

When I pulled into the lot where the police had towed my car and saw the shape it was in, I felt nauseous.

It was a miracle Ali was still alive. The airbags were probably what had saved her; if she were a larger person, her skull might've been crushed, judging by the way the roof of the car had buckled.

I gripped the steering wheel when the ramifications of that thought tore through me like a gale-force wind. *If she were a larger person—like me—her skull might've been crushed. Jesus fucking Christ.* Ali was driving my car. My car. The one I should've been driving.

She'd also said that the guy who "gave her the creeps," was standing by my car.

Ali's accident had been intentional, except I was supposed to be behind the wheel. That meant someone had figured out my carefully crafted plan and was attempting to stop me before I could execute it. Given there was one person the plan was intended to take down, I now knew that the hook I'd baited caught the fish. I just had to pay close attention to what he did next.

I pulled out my cell phone and called my boss. Money answered on the first ring.

"Cope?"

"Hello, sir. I'm sure by now you've heard about the accident this morning, involving an *Express* reporter who was driving my car."

"I have."

"The reason for my call is to let you know I'll be taking a leave of absence from all other cases on my roster. I will, however, still continue to oversee Warrick's trial."

He cleared his throat. "Why don't you come into the office tomorrow, and we'll discuss this further?"

"I won't be able to do that, sir."

"Why not?"

"Because I believe the accident that almost killed Ali Graham was intended for me. Until I figure out who was behind it, I'll be operating independently."

"That isn't your decision to make, Cope."

"No? The alternative, then, would be to fire me."

"There's no need to overreact. All I'm saying is I want you to come into the office so we can discuss this in person."

"And all I'm saying is no." I disconnected the call, turned off my cell, and tossed it on the passenger seat.

I'd thrown down the gauntlet; now I'd sit back and watch who from the agency responded and how.

I stopped by the café before going up to my apartment. While I waited for my order, I told Lindsey about Ali's accident. She came around and sat at one of the high tops, motioning for me to join her.

"Talk to me, Cope," she said. "What's with you and this woman? First you order enough food to feed her for a week, now you're telling me she's in the hospital and you've been there with her most of the day."

I shrugged. "I thought you'd want to know."

"That's not my point. Two days ago, you didn't know her. Now you're her knight in shining armor. What's that about?"

"She doesn't know anyone in DC or even in the area."

Lindsey sat back in the stool and folded her arms. "And this is all your responsibility because…"

"Because she is damn fine-lookin'," said one of the cooks from the back.

"There is that," Lindsey said, tapping her cheek with her finger. "But I think there's more to it."

I turned my head and looked out the window over at the building I now thought of as Ali's. "If you figure out what, please tell me," I murmured.

I took my food order upstairs and called Stella. Even if she was pissed at me, she'd still answer if only for an update on Ali.

When I finished telling her my plan, she was silent. "What's up, Stell?"

"I would've given anything for someone to do this for me when I was first starting out."

"But?"

"How much do you know about her? What's her background report say?"

Everything appeared to be on the up-and-up. Both her parents had died within a year of each other when she was a teenager. There was a settlement involved in her father's death, which she had used to attend Northwestern University, where she earned a master's degree in journalism.

"Doesn't it strike you as odd that the *Express* would've assigned a brand new reporter to the Warrick trial?"

It hadn't at all, actually. Most espionage cases, particularly when someone from inside the CIA was on trial, were settled without fanfare. Details of the outcome were sealed up tight, leaving nothing for anyone to report. "It surprised me more that you were there," I told her. "Why are you covering it?"

"Because I'm fucking good at what I do, Cope, and if you think for one second I don't know there's more to what's happening with Warrick than meets the eye, then you should consider resigning from your job."

"Maybe the higher-ups at the *Express* aren't as good as you are."

"No need to blow smoke up my ass. All I'm saying is everything with Ali doesn't quite add up for me. If you aren't feeling the same way, maybe you better give it some thought."

I had one more person to contact before I called it a night. Considering the man I was trying to reach was in part of the country that was behind us by a couple of hours, I didn't bother to check the time.

"Hey, Decker," I said when he answered.

"Cope, I hope you're going to tell me there's been some movement."

"There was an accident earlier today. Someone driving my car was almost killed."

"I'd say that was movement. He's getting nervous, Cope. Nervous means sloppy."

"It can also mean deadly. We need more bubble wrap around Irish."

"I'll take care of it. What about you?"

"What do you mean?"

"You were almost killed this morning, Cope. What's the condition of the person who was driving your car."

"Amazingly, she only broke her arm and bruised some ribs."

"She?"

"Long story, but a reporter covering Warrick's trial."

"Think she's in any kind of danger? Or are you thinking wrong place, wrong time?"

"Wrong place, wrong time."

"Roger that. Give me a few minutes to add to the crew, and I'll get back to you."

Decker Ashford was one of the founding partners in a private covert ops firm called the Invincible

Intelligence and Security Group. The other partners were former MI6 agents, who I'd worked many ops with over the years. They'd also added former agents, some of whom I'd handled, to their roster of contractors.

While Decker had always maintained contractor status with the CIA, he and I had worked several missions together.

It was on one of those ops that he poked his nose into what Irish and I were doing. I had two choices: blow the whole mission up, or bring Decker into the fold. I chose the latter.

In the same way Irish trusted me, I trusted Decker, and by association, the rest of the Invincibles team. That included Hammer. As far as the CIA was concerned, he was acting as a trial consultant. What he was really doing was watching my back as well as Warrick's.

Another of Decker's team, Garrett "Rage" Williams, was currently undercover as Irish's cellmate, and by tomorrow morning, I knew Decker would have two more men assigned, who would stay in lockup, protecting Warrick as long as he was there. Additionally, I knew he'd send at least two my way.

Fifteen minutes later, Decker called back. "I'm sending Ritter Johnson and Roscoe Wheaton in. They'll report to you in the morning. Hammer and Rage will keep their eyes and ears open as will the new team members. If any of them feels like you or they need more support, they'll ask for it."

"Appreciate this, Deck." Both Ritter "Rock" Johnson and Roscoe "Buck" Wheaton had once been with the agency but now worked for the Invincibles, just like Hammer and Rage did.

"By the way, I've got reports headed your way. Anyone other than the names you've already given me that you want me to run?"

Decker Ashford could find anything on anybody. No matter how good their cover, he was capable of going deeper than any other organization, and that included the CIA, the NSA, SIS, and Russian intelligence.

Ali Graham. Her name was on the tip of my tongue. Especially after Stella's warning. I hung up without saying it, though.

My alarm went off two hours after I went to sleep, but instead of hitting the snooze button, I got up. After a cup of triple-shot espresso, I climbed on the exercise bike that sat in the front of my apartment and loaded up a workout.

Most days, I did the interactive option, but today I just went with one that was pre-programmed. From where I was on mine, I could see the one sitting, unused, in Ali's apartment. I couldn't explain why I was so obsessed with her getting on it. I guess I wanted to see her conquer her fear of heights and enjoy the space in the way it was designed to be lived in.

Just as I finished, a light in her place came on. Seconds later, Chloe walked over to the window and waved. I wiped the sweat from my face with a towel and waved back. She put her hand to her ear, mimicking a phone, and I nodded and went in search of mine. When I found it, it was vibrating with her call.

"You're up early," I said, remembering she was from the West Coast.

"Ali had a bad night—"

"What happened?"

"She couldn't sleep, so I stayed with her. I got back here a few minutes ago."

"How was she doing when you left?"

"The resident on night duty finally told her that if she didn't start using the pain-med delivery, he was going to have it given to her."

"Why wasn't she using it?"

"You know Ali." She paused. "Actually, you don't, do you? She can be…stubborn."

"She can't heal if she doesn't sleep."

"Can I ask you something?"

"Sure."

"Why are you so vested in her recovery? Not just her recovery. In Ali?"

That was the million-dollar question everyone kept asking.

9

Ali

My phone was sitting out of my reach on the table where they set my breakfast. If you could call it breakfast. As the morning nurse had said when she came in to introduce herself, chicken broth and cherry gelatin this early in the morning would ruin the appetite of a starving person.

When I tried leaning forward to get my cell, level-ten pain shot through me. I hit the button that delivered morphine once and then figured, as much as they were pestering me to use it, I'd do it again. Seconds later, the nurse came back in.

"Bad this morning?" she asked.

"I tried to get my phone."

"You know what this is for, right?" She set the combination television remote, bed adjuster, call button in my hand before moving my cell within reach.

"I'm not very good at asking for help." The door opened, and Cope walked in, carrying a beverage tray and a bag.

"Coffee delivery?" the nurse asked, wiggling her eyebrows.

Cope picked up the silver dome covering my chicken broth and set it back down. "Yuck."

The nurse nodded her head at his bag. "Whatever is in there, she can't eat. Not yet. Maybe after the doctor sees her."

"What about me?" asked the doctor I recognized from the emergency room.

I rested my head against the pillow and closed my eyes. After not sleeping last night, it was all I wanted to do now. Given the pain was subsiding, I assumed the morphine had something to do with my drowsiness. I wished all these people would leave, so I could rest.

I felt Cope's fingers brush the hair from my forehead. It was something I was growing accustomed to, and that was just weird. I opened my eyes and looked into his.

"Chloe said you had a hard night."

"Couldn't sleep," I murmured.

"I would say you have to stay on a liquid diet and confiscate whatever goodness is in this bag," said the doctor, "but that would just be cruel." He took a look at the monitors and checked my pulse. "I will need you to step out, young man," he said to Cope.

"You can head out if you need to," I told him, garnering raised eyebrows from him and the nurse. "Thanks for the coffee."

Cope stood where he was, staring at me as though he wanted to say something but couldn't find the words. Was it my imagination, or did he look hurt?

"I'll come back in when the doctor's finished."

I breathed a sigh of relief when the door closed behind him.

"Trouble in paradise?" the doctor asked. "Take a deep breath," he said, not waiting for me to answer his question.

"I don't even know him," I mumbled when he moved the stethoscope away from my chest.

"Have you remembered anything about the accident?"

"Bits and pieces." It was part of the reason I couldn't sleep. Every time I drifted off, I could see the car barreling toward me.

"If that's the case, I don't see any reason you can't go home today." The doctor typed something on the keyboard of a laptop and motioned with his head toward the door. "If he's your ride, I can speed up your release."

Was he? Would it be silly—not to mention, rude—if I called Chloe and asked her to come all the way back here, especially since she'd spent the night with me? "That would be great. Thanks," I said when the doctor walked out.

Before Cope came back in, I needed to call Jessica and let her know I was being released from the hospital. When we spoke briefly last night, she hadn't yet decided how she wanted me to proceed; however, she found Cope's constant attention a win.

"Can I get you anything else right now?" the nurse asked.

My ringing cell startled me. "Um, actually, if the guy who was in here earlier is still out there, could you ask him to wait a few more minutes before coming in?"

She gave me the thumbs up and walked out.

"How are you feeling this morning?" Jessica asked when I answered.

"The doctor just left. He said I can go home today."

"Good news. What's your plan?"

"You tell me."

"Has Cope said anything more about feeding you reports on the trial?"

"We haven't had a chance to talk this morning. Right after he got here, the doctor came in."

"He's there?"

"Out in the hallway, but yeah."

"Roll with it, Ali."

"Understood." I set my phone down and rested my head against the pillow. I knew Jessica would be happy when I told her Cope was here. There was something else I hadn't told her, and if I had, she would not have been the slightest bit pleased. She'd be furious to the point of pulling me off the assignment if she knew how hard I was falling for the man who had just rapped on the door, asking if he could come back in.

"The doctor said I can break you out of here."

Before I could respond, the nurse from earlier returned. "The doctor had one more question before he signs off on letting you go home." She looked between Cope and me. "I need you to assure me you're not going to be there on your own. For an hour or two, it's okay, but not longer than that. Do you have someone who—"

"I'll be with her."

"What?" I gasped and then put my hand on my side, where a stabbing pain shot through me. "No, my friend…she's in town…staying with me."

"Okay, as long as there's someone. I'll be back in a few minutes."

"Why did you say that?" I asked between shallow breaths.

"Because if you need someone with you, I can be that person."

I shook my head. "You can't. The trial."

"I'll figure something out."

"Cope?"

When he took my hand in his, I couldn't deny the zing of electricity that flowed through me, but what I had to say was important. "You're a nice guy, but this—me—isn't your responsibility. I honestly don't know why you feel like it is. Whatever you think you need to atone for, you don't. I'm a big girl and I'll be fine."

I held up one finger when my cell rang and I saw it was Chloe calling. "I thought you'd be asleep," I answered.

"I would be, but there's a problem, sweetie. I know I just got here, but one of my employees has appendicitis and has to have emergency surgery. I'm so sorry to do this, but I need to fly home as soon as I can catch a flight."

"Don't apologize, Chloe. Do what you need to do. I'll be fine."

"What's wrong?" Cope asked when I ended the call.

I bit my bottom lip, wishing I didn't have to tell him that my friend had to leave already. "Chloe owns a grooming and pet-sitting business. One of her employees has to have surgery, so she has to go home."

He nodded in a way that made me wish I had *anyone* else I could call. I hated being pitied, and the look on his face was all about feeling sorry for me.

"Fuck," I mumbled under my breath.

Cope pulled his hand away and stood so abruptly that it startled me. "Here's the thing, Ali. If I'm so offensive to you, then sure, do this on your own."

I was stunned, which quickly morphed into feeling like an absolute shit. "Wait," I said when he put his hand on the doorknob. "I'm sorry."

He didn't walk out, but he didn't speak or even look at me.

"I'm trying to let you off the hook, not insult you."

He turned around then. "Just let me do this." His voice spoke directly to my heart.

"Okay," I whispered.

He let out a breath and walked back over to me.

"I didn't mean to hurt your feelings."

He sat down and looked into my eyes. "You did, so you'll have to make it up to me."

"Yeah?"

"Yeah."

I wondered what he had in mind. Gauging by the heat in his eyes, I could guess. The last thing I should be doing was hoping.

10

Cope

I'd expected my little spitfire—the way I'd begun referring to Ali in my mind—to have a fit when I took her to my apartment instead of hers. She didn't disappoint. However, the trip from the hospital here had done her in.

"I can walk, Cope," she'd argued when I pulled a wheelchair I'd borrowed out of the trunk.

"You sure about that?" I'd bruised some ribs playing football and remembered they hurt like hell.

She turned to get out of the car, and even that was too much.

"Ready?" I asked, standing with my hands on my hips.

When she glared at me, I laughed and brought the wheelchair closer.

She was so exhausted by the time we got upstairs, that she didn't have the strength to complain when I wheeled her into what was obviously my bedroom rather than the guest room.

When we got the final okay to leave the hospital, I'd gone ahead of Ali and the nurse wheeling her downstairs, and brought my rental around to the entrance. I used that time to call the one woman I knew would help me without asking questions—my mother.

Not that she never would. Eventually, she'd fire them at me faster than an M134 Minigun. However, she'd wait until after she did everything I'd asked.

Laurel Margaret Browning-Copeland was a graduate of Bryn Mawr, where she'd parlayed her degree in political science into becoming a senator's wife. I sometimes wondered if my father's campaigns and subsequent career would have been successful had he married someone else. The two shared a bond I envied. They'd met when she was a sophomore at her alma mater and my father was a grad student at nearby Villanova. Their courtship was the stuff of fairy tales, and clearly, my mother thought of my father as her very own Prince Charming. While many political couples put that face forward in public, having spent eighteen years growing up in their home, I knew firsthand that their love story was authentic.

"Can I help?" my mom asked, coming into the room where I was trying to figure out how best to get Ali from the wheelchair onto the bed.

"By the way, I'm Laurel, Sumner's mother." She walked around the chair, sat on the bed, and held her hand out.

"Nice to meet you. I'm Ali Graham. Sumner's charity case."

My mother smiled and put her hand on the arm of the wheelchair. "Sumner, if you put this down, you can reach around and gather Ali in your arms. Which side is the worst, sweetheart?"

"The right," Ali answered. My mom put the other arm down and directed me to come around to the opposite side.

"She just said the right hurt the worst." My mother pointed to Ali's left arm. "Good point," I mumbled, feeling like a jackass. "Ready?" I asked, putting one arm behind her knees and the other around her back. I swept her up as gently as I could and then rested her body against the wall of pillows my mother was tucking in around her.

"How's that?" she asked.

"It's fine," Ali grunted, trying to adjust her body into a comfortable position.

"Where are her pain meds?" my mom asked.

"Kitchen."

She put her hands on her hips and glared at me. "Don't just stand there. Go get them."

I could hear them talking as I rushed off, but not what either was saying. No doubt, my mother knew the exact right words to put Ali at ease, and for that, I was grateful.

I hurried back, bottle of pills and glass of water in hand, and saw the door was closed. Seconds later, it opened, and my mother reached her hand out. "That's all for now, Sumner," she said, closing it again as I stood stupefied.

Not knowing what else to do, I went back to the kitchen, opened the refrigerator, grabbed a beer, and walked over to the window. The streets below were crowded with people no doubt rushing to get lunch during the mid-day break. Every so often, a runner would weave their way through the crowd or a bicyclist would whiz past the cars stuck in traffic gridlock.

How long had it been since I did any exercise outside? I couldn't remember. Maybe that's why, when I saw the bike in the window of the building across the way, I'd gone out and bought my own. At least I could look out to where there was fresh air, even if it wasn't blowing in my face.

"She's asleep." My mother's voice was soft.

"Thanks for coming over, Mom."

She put her hand on my shoulder and leaned against me. "She seems nice."

I waited for a barrage of questions that didn't come. Instead, after a few minutes, my mother asked if I thought I'd be okay on my own. After I assured her I would be, she left, leaving me feeling perplexed.

I pulled out my laptop and sat on the stool at my kitchen counter. I needed to get a message to Warrick. I knew him well enough to predict he was in full panic mode. I was just about to call Hammer when I got a message from one of the men Decker had assigned.

In position, the text message read.

Copy, I responded and pulled up Hammer's number.

"Hey, Cope."

"How's Irish?"

"Fucking pussy," Hammer muttered.

It was an opinion many in the intelligence community shared, but it wasn't a fair one. Until recently, no one but Irish and me knew exactly what I'd asked the man to undertake for the last seven years. Upon his arrest, Warrick had been vilified from every direction, and yet he hadn't cracked. Even to Rage, who was the Invincibles' man on the inside, making sure no one could get to him.

"Tell him I'll get with him as soon as I can."

"You got it. Anything else?"

I wanted to tell Hammer to reassure Irish, but that would only piss him off more. The last thing Irish needed was the attorney giving him shit.

No one knew Irish better than I did, inside the CIA or out.

He and I met at Camp Peary—known within the agency as "The Farm"—where we both underwent training for the Clandestine Service Division. We'd spent eighteen months at the highly classified, nine-thousand-acre military camp where the lead instructor was known for telling every new recruit, "It doesn't matter who you used to be or who you are. All that matters is who we teach you to be."

Irish had arrived a couple of months before I did, but lagged behind me in his completion of several of the milestones. When I was approached to become his training partner, I didn't know what they really had in mind was for me to become his handler.

In hindsight, it was easy for me to understand why the company had chosen that role for me rather than put me out in the field. I'd been too green back then to realize the kinds of risks that would present themselves if it became known who my father was.

From then on, Irish and I were a team in a way I never had been with the other agents I handled. It was probably harder on me than it was on Warrick, when people like Hammer gave him shit. I was the one who'd created the reputation he had, and it had served us well in the missions we'd run together.

The mission now, though, outweighed every other and was dependent upon Irish being able to hold his shit together without my constant attention.

By three in the afternoon, I was hungry. I eased my bedroom door open and was relieved to find Ali still asleep, especially after what Chloe had said about her not getting any rest last night.

Rather than going downstairs and placing my order in person, I called the café. "Hey, Cope, how's the patient?" Lindsey asked.

"Asleep for now, but when she wakes up, she's going to be as hungry as I am." The line was quiet on the other end. "Linds?"

"I'm here. Don't get me wrong, I really appreciate your business, but…doesn't the hospital have food? Or isn't there somewhere closer you can pick something up?"

"We're here. She was released this morning."

"Here?"

"Upstairs."

"In your apartment?"

"Lindsey? What the hell? *Yes!* Now can I order some food?"

"Don't get your tighty-whities all bunched up. I'm surprised is all."

After I placed my order, Lindsey offered to have the food delivered so I didn't have to leave Ali alone. When I opened the door thirty minutes later, I didn't expect to see her standing on the other side of it.

Rather than invite her in, I took the bags out of her hands, eased the door closed with my foot, and told her I'd be right back. She had her arms folded when I handed her cash for the food. "Who's got their tighty-whities in a bunch now?" I said when she didn't take the money from me.

She grabbed the bills from my hand and spun around toward the elevator without another word. "Keep the change," I called out after her.

When I walked into the kitchen and found Ali standing at the counter, looking white as a ghost, I rushed over to her. "What are you doing out of bed?"

"I had to…you know…use the bathroom."

"Maybe you should sit down." I pulled the stool I'd been sitting on out and turned it so she could lean into it. It was the perfect height that she didn't have to bend down or climb up.

"That smells really good."

I smiled and winked. "I got all your favorites."

She smiled too, at least briefly, reminding me that she probably needed another pain pill. I grabbed the bottle, set it in front of her, and poured a glass of water.

When I turned back around, she was looking at my laptop.

"Sorry," she muttered when our eyes met. "Don't worry, I can't see anything. I don't have my contacts in, and I have no idea where my glasses are."

Contacts? Glasses? "When's the last time you had them?"

"Which?"

"Let's start with your glasses since they'll be easier to find."

"Yesterday morning. Wait. What day is it?"

"You haven't missed any. It's Wednesday."

"I left them in the apartment."

"I can go get them for you."

She eased forward and put her head in her hand. "I need more than my glasses, Cope." Her eyes opened wide. "Where's *my* laptop? And my purse? And my phone? And my wallet? *Shit!*"

It dawned on me that the bag of stuff she took with her from the hospital didn't have much in it. "Did Chloe take it all back to your apartment?"

Her shoulders relaxed. "She did. I remember her saying she was going to this morning. I think she said she was leaving my phone and wallet, though."

"Be right back." I rushed into the room where I'd set the bag and carried it out to her. "Might be in here."

She rummaged through it and set both items on the counter. "That's a relief," she mumbled.

I noticed the bottle of pills sat unopened. "You better take one of those."

"I don't like feeling so out of it."

I opened the bottle and handed her one. "If you don't take it, you'll feel way more than out of it." I started taking food out of the bags, but out of the corner of my eye, I saw Ali stick her tongue out at me. If her ribs weren't bruised and her arm wasn't broken, she'd pay for that. I should start keeping track. I had to turn my back when the ideas I had for punishing her went straight from my brain to my cock.

I'd lied when I said I got all her favorites from the café; I'd gotten mine. But based on how much she ate, Ali must've liked what I chose.

"What do you say we take a quick trip over to your apartment before you crash for the night?"

She raised a brow, but was smiling.

"Sorry, poor choice of words."

By the time I wheeled her across the street, I realized what a bad idea this was. No matter how small the bump, Ali felt it. She didn't complain, but I saw every wince. Even the elevator doors closing and then opening jarred her.

I wheeled her to the apartment door, used the key card to open it, and wondered if it might be better if she stayed here tonight.

"Hey, I was thinking…" She went ghost-white again. "What is it? Pain?"

She shook her head. "Someone's been in here."

We'd only gotten as far as the kitchen, but nothing appeared amiss. "Your friend was, right?"

"Someone else."

Given the look on her face, I knelt down beside her and put my hand on the arm of the wheelchair. "What makes you say that?"

"Take a deep breath."

I did and then shook my head.

"Cologne."

"Could it be—"

"If you're going to ask if it could be Chloe's, the answer is no. She's worn the same perfume all the years I've known her. If she'd switched, I would've noticed. Besides, what I smell is men's cologne, not perfume."

I took another whiff, but I couldn't smell anything. I wasn't taking any chances, though. "I think it's your imagination," I said, louder than I needed to, shaking my head and putting my finger in front of my mouth so she didn't respond. As quietly as I could, I wheeled her back out and into the elevator.

"Where are we going?" she asked once the door closed behind us.

"I'm taking you back to my place until I can confirm that whomever's cologne you smelled isn't still in there."

"It was familiar."

"And you're sure it couldn't be from Chloe?"

Ali shot me a glare, but by the time I wheeled her into my apartment, she looked like she couldn't keep her eyes open a minute longer. I took her straight into the bedroom, lowered the side of the wheelchair, and lifted her onto the bed.

"Before you nod off, tell me what all you want me to get."

"It'll be easier if you just grab my bag and my suitcase. I didn't unpack."

I'd ask why later. First, I wanted to get over there and make sure there wasn't anyone still in the apartment. "Is your phone on?"

Ali nodded.

"Make sure the ringer's on and turn the volume up, in case I have questions."

She nodded again, as though that was all she had energy for. I brushed her hair from her forehead. "I'll be back as soon as I can." Before I realized what I was doing, my lips touched hers. Kissing her before I left, especially with her stretched out on my bed, seemed like such a natural thing to do.

"I'm sorry, Ali," I whispered, resting my forehead against hers. "There's just something—"

"Do it again."

I pulled back and looked into her eyes. "What did you say?"

"Kiss me again, Cope."

Once the invitation was out there, I had to RSVP. I brought my hand to her cheek and stroked her lower lip with my thumb until her mouth opened enough for me to see the tip of her tongue. I leaned forward and touched it with the tip of mine. Ali's right hand moved to my leg, and her fingers dug into my muscle when I went in deeper. I held myself back, so afraid I'd hurt her if I kissed her the way I'd been longing to.

I knew I had to leave, but my body wasn't going anywhere, especially when she angled her head and I heard her moan softly. *Wait.* She moaned.

I wrenched my mouth from hers and looked into her eyes. "Did I hurt you?"

She shook her head and bit her lower lip. Her eyes were hooded, her cheeks were flushed, and her pebbled nipples were like little beacons, begging for my tongue to lick them. I closed my eyes and looked up at the ceiling. The woman in my bed was recovering from a car accident, I reminded myself more than once. Which meant the body I longed to have naked beneath mine was off-limits. I moaned like she had, kissed her once more, and then pulled away and stood.

"I'll be back as soon as I can," I repeated, this time without the kiss.

"Cope?" she said when I was about to walk out the bedroom door.

I turned around. "Yeah?"

"Be careful."

"Always. Keep your phone close by." I raced out and into the elevator, and out of my building.

"What's up, Cope?" asked Buck. While Ali hadn't seen him or Rock, I knew they'd been nearby when I took her across the street and again when I brought her back.

"Ali thinks someone was in the apartment."

"Was or is?"

"Both. Let's go."

Rock was there, waiting for us when we got back across the street.

"Cope," he said quietly.

I nodded, put the key card in the slot, and opened the door. What I saw when I walked in, confirmed that there had, in fact, been someone in here earlier when Ali and I were.

"Holy shit," whispered Buck as the three of us went in different directions, clearing each room.

11

Ali

As hard as it was for me to keep my eyes open, I couldn't sleep until I heard something from Cope. The fact that he'd been gone for more than thirty minutes was beginning to worry me.

I picked up my phone for the countless time, stupidly wondering if I'd missed a call from him. I eased myself off the bed and slowly walked out into the main living area. Even from the hallway, I could tell lights were on in the apartment I'd only spent two nights in.

"You can do this," I whispered to myself as I crept closer to the windows. I rested my hand on the back of Cope's sofa and took as deep a breath as I could without it hurting and then took two more steps forward.

I gasped when I saw the activity taking place in the loft, but nearly screamed when I heard the lock on the door behind me click.

"What are you doing out of bed?" Cope asked, rushing over to me.

"I was worried."

He smiled and brushed my chin with his fingertip. "I guess so. Look at where you are."

I didn't have to look. I already knew I'd gotten closer to the windows than I was willing to before. "What's going on over there?" I asked, motioning with my head.

"You were right. Someone was in there."

"Who are all those people?"

"They're from the agency. Let's get you back in bed."

Cope went off to get the wheelchair while I kept watching the shadows of the people in the apartment across the street.

"Where are my bags?" I asked when he came back and helped me into the chair.

"Someone will bring them over shortly."

"Why didn't you?"

"The guys are still gathering evidence."

He wheeled me into the bedroom and helped me get back into bed.

"There's a lot you aren't telling me."

He scrubbed his face with his hand. "There's a lot I don't know." He walked to the door but hesitated and leaned his back against the jamb. "We'll talk more tomorrow. Do you need anything?"

I nodded slowly and he smiled. "I'm almost afraid to ask."

"Stay with me."

The smile left his face, and I held my breath. He closed the door, walked around the bed, and stretched out beside me.

"What did you think I was going to say?"

"That you wanted the last two pieces of baklava."

"That you ate?"

He nodded and smiled sheepishly.

"I'd rather you kiss me again."

He raised a brow, and I had to admit, I wasn't normally quite so…forward. Or stupid. I had no business starting a physical relationship with this man, but I couldn't help myself. Maybe it was the pain meds, or maybe it was just Cope. I wanted to feel his lips on mine more than I wanted dessert—or in the heat of this moment—to do my job.

"Pretty demanding," he murmured, with his head above mine. "I like that." He leaned forward and kissed me, tentatively at first, like he had earlier, but it quickly deepened. His tongue snaked its way into my mouth, exploring in the same way I wished I could explore his body with my hands. I raised my left arm; I didn't feel any pain, so I lifted the hem of my shirt.

When he noticed what I was doing, he stopped kissing me and watched. He gasped when he saw I didn't have a bra on and my breasts were exposed. Without putting any weight on my body, he leaned forward and swirled his tongue around my nipple. He scooted his body back and moved my blouse away from my side, kissing the skin beneath. "You're bruised," he murmured, running his fingertips over the part of my body that hurt the worst.

"Ali," he whispered, gently kissing the places where his fingertips had just been. "I'm so afraid I'm going to hurt you."

"You won't," I whispered back.

His hand came back to my breast, as did his mouth. Knowing that if I moved, pain would shoot through my body, I stayed as still as I could. It was almost as though he'd restrained me. The idea alone drenched my panties.

"What was that thought, Ali?" He raised his head just slightly, so he could look into my eyes. "Tell me," he demanded with a grin.

"I can't move."

His pupils flared. "I see. So the idea of being forced to take all the pleasure I give you, gets you wet?" Without hesitation, he reached between my legs, cupping my mound through my yoga pants.

"You're soaked," he muttered, increasing the pressure at the base of his palm. "Do you know how hard that makes me?" I wanted to find out for myself, but I knew if I reached for him, it would hurt, and then he'd stop. "Where else are you bruised? I need to know where I can touch you, Ali."

"Help me get my pants off," I murmured, hoping I wasn't pushing too hard too fast.

He shifted his body down the bed, sat up, and put his hands on my waistband. "I'm going to do this slowly."

I nodded and rested my hand on his. He worked his fingers between my pants and my skin, and as promised, he slowly pulled the fabric over my ass. They were as far down as my bikini line when he stopped.

"Are you sure about this?"

"Yes," I breathed, wondering if the pain medicine had an aphrodisiac in it. I'd never wanted to feel a man's touch more than Cope's.

He gently pulled the stretchy fabric farther down until he could easily slip my pants off my legs.

"What about my panties?"

With heated eyes, he looked up at me. "I'm human, Ali. You can only tempt me so much before I lose my restraint."

He ran his hands over my legs, gently pushing my thighs apart and kissing the inside of my knee. It was all I could do not to arch my back and push my pussy toward his face. I was a quick learner, though, and knew the pleasure would not be worth the pain.

"Tell me where else it hurts," he murmured.

"Right now? Nowhere."

"Feeling no pain, eh? I hope you don't regret this tomorrow." He leaned forward again, kissed my knee-cap, and then straightened out next to me.

"Sleep, Ali. The quicker you heal, the sooner I can explore the rest of your body."

I clenched my fist in frustration, not knowing how in the hell he could turn his desire off that quickly.

"Just in case you're wondering, there are parts of my body that hurt worse than any parts of yours do right now."

"Why did you stop?"

It took him so long to answer that I thought maybe he'd fallen asleep, but his eyes were open.

He took a deep breath and turned on his side. "I want you, Ali. All of you. I think I have since you called me a muscle-bound asshole, which seems like weeks ago, but in reality, it's only been a couple of days. The point is, I want all of you. I don't want to hold back when we're together—and just in case you're questioning whether we will be—I promise you that, as soon as I know I won't hurt you, I'll have as much of my body touching yours as is physically possible."

When I woke the next morning, I was alone in bed, but I could hear Cope's voice from the other room. I tried not to listen to what I assumed was a private conversation, but when he raised his voice in anger, there was no way not to hear him.

"Not good enough. Get a subpoena if you have to, but I want to see the security footage no later than nine." He paused. "Yes, I do realize that is less than an hour from now. Do your fucking job and get it."

I heard his footsteps coming in my direction, and then the door opened. "You're awake."

"You're angry."

He sat next to me on the bed. "Frustrated."

"I know the feeling." I was teasing and hoped he took it that way. He smiled.

"Your bag arrived earlier, but I have to warn you, your laptop didn't."

I bit my bottom lip. "Why not?"

"We couldn't find it in the apartment." He studied me. "You don't seem very upset by that news."

"Apart from needing to get a replacement, it doesn't matter much." There was nothing on it that would give away who I really was to Cope or anyone else.

"What about your…work?"

"I don't keep anything on my laptop. I would think a CIA agent would understand why not." I winked, and that seemed to finally disarm him.

"I do. It's just that most people aren't as practical… or smart."

"I'd, um, really like to shower. If that's okay."

He stood. "Of course it is. Do you need help?"

I would like it, but wasn't sure I'd need it. "I'll be okay. I just have to wrap this." I raised my left arm just slightly, which hurt like a son-of-a-bitch.

Cope nodded. "I'll get your bag and…a bag."

By the time I finished showering, the pain pill I took when I woke up had kicked in full force. I wasn't sure how I'd managed to get undressed, but the reverse seemed impossible. I could probably get my panties on and maybe my pants, but it wouldn't be easy. I sat down on the toilet seat and thought about my predicament.

"Everything okay in there?" Cope asked from the other side of the door a few minutes later.

"Um…" *Gawd*, this was so embarrassing.

"Ali?"

"I'm having trouble getting dressed." As soon as the words left my mouth, I could feel the heat flush my cheeks.

"Can I help?"

It wasn't as though the man hadn't seen my boobs. In fact, last night, I'd wanted him to see a hell of a lot more than that. "If you wouldn't mind."

The door creaked open slowly, and he peeked around it. I remembered thinking he looked like he could be a politician when I first saw him at the court-house. This morning, he was all Boy Scout with his closely-cropped, slicked-back hair and eager-to-please look in his eyes.

He picked up the black lace panties sitting near the sink. "Should we start with these?"

"Sure." He knelt in front of me and untucked the towel covering most of my body.

"Lift for me." With his help, I shimmied into my panties. His gaze rested on my puckered nipples, and when he leaned forward, I thought he might take one into his mouth. I hissed in a breath when, instead, he trapped one between the tips of two fingers. My head dropped back, and his mouth landed on my neck, the hard tip of his tongue swirling small circles up to the place right below my ear.

"Is this okay?" he murmured.

I answered by bringing his hand to my other breast. He leaned back, looked into my eyes, and dangled my bra from the tip of his finger that was no longer toying with my nipple.

"I'm not sure wearing this would be a good idea."

"Okay," I mumbled, wishing he'd put his hands and lips back on my body.

"I'll be right back." He stood and walked out of the bathroom. I'd stand too and follow him, but my legs were shaking. When he came back, he had a sweatshirt in his hand. "This will swim on you, but it'll be easier to get over your cast."

He put it over my head and stretched the arm out until my broken one was covered.

"Just one more…" he said, and I held my right arm out to him. Instead of putting the sweatshirt on it, he captured my nipple between his teeth. His tongue swirled around and around it until I cried out. Cope released it with a pop. "I needed another taste." He put the sweatshirt over my head and pulled it down so it covered my body. "Anything else I can help with?" he asked, standing. He walked out without waiting for my answer.

"Look at you," he said when I walked into the kitchen and he looked up from his computer. "Feel better?"

"Not really."

He smirked. "What can I get you? Coffee?"

"Bucketloads if you have it."

He handed me a cup with cream, no sugar. "Hungry?"

"Famished."

He opened the refrigerator and leaned over to look inside, giving me a perfect view of the way his jeans stretched over his tight ass. The muscles of his arm holding the door open, flexed.

"What do you bench press?" I asked.

He turned around and put a carton of eggs on the counter. "Depends on what I'm training for. What about you?"

"Same."

"Why'd you ask?"

"You're in really good shape."

His cheeks flushed, which surprised me. "So are you."

"You're also really pretty."

Cope laughed. "So are you."

"Yeah, I kinda handed you that one."

I watched as he cracked ten eggs into a bowl. "I only know how to make them scrambled," he said when he looked up and saw me watching.

"Those better not all be for me."

"I've seen you eat. You can polish these off in a hot minute."

"Very funny. So…do you need to go to work or something today?"

"Working from home, but tomorrow is a different story. I'll probably be gone most of the day. I've, um, asked my mother to come over."

I rolled my eyes. "That's sweet, but not necessary." Not to mention, I didn't feel right about getting to know Cope's mother or anyone else in his family. Spending time alone with him like I was, was bad enough.

"The nurse said you can't be alone for more than a couple of hours."

"I'm sure she was exaggerating. I'll be fine."

He shook his head. "I won't be."

"What do you mean?"

"Instead of getting done what I need to, I'll worry about you."

"I've been on my own for a really long time, I can take care—"

He leaned forward and rested his elbows on the counter. His face was only a few inches from mine. "I'll worry about you." When his cell phone vibrated, he reached over and picked it up. "Rock's here," he said after setting the phone back down on the counter.

"Rock?"

"You'll see."

When he opened the door of his apartment, the man standing on the other side of it could've been a stunt double for Dwayne Johnson.

When Cope introduced him as Ritter Johnson, I wondered if he and his doppelganger were related.

He set a bag on the counter. "I'm pretty sure this is for you."

I scrunched my eyes and looked at Cope.

"Open it," he prodded.

I pulled out a box containing a brand new version of the same kind of computer that was taken from the apartment. I looked up at Cope a second time.

"You need to work," he muttered.

"Where did this come from?"

"I'm just going to wait over here," said Rock, walking over to the windows.

"I asked Rock to pick it up and bring it to you."

I looked in the bag and didn't see a receipt. "How much do I owe you?"

"Don't worry about it."

My eyes opened wide. "You can't buy me a computer, Cope."

"It was that or let you borrow one of mine, and that's against regulations."

"Ha, ha." I ran my hand over the white box covered in plastic wrap. I hadn't let the idea of being "disconnected" settle in, but if I had, I certainly would've been agitated by it. "Thank you, but I insist on reimbursing you for this as soon as I have the energy to go get my wallet."

"We can work it out later," he said, motioning with his head toward Rock.

"Sure. Of course." I shifted to stand, and Cope came around from the other side of the counter.

"Where are you going?"

"I'm giving you some privacy."

"We might need you." Cope turned to Rock. "Do you have it?"

He nodded and patted his pocket. "Right here."

"Bring it over."

Cope opened his laptop and inserted the thumb drive that Rock handed to him. I could tell that he played a video recording, but without my glasses, I couldn't see much of anything other than shapes moving around on the screen. He hit the space bar and turned the computer toward me. "Is this the guy you saw in the parking garage?"

I looked from the screen to him. "Without my glasses, I can't tell."

"I'll get them. Where are they?"

"In my bag." I didn't like not being able to do something as simple as getting my glasses, but if he went, it would be much faster.

"These them?" he asked, what seemed like seconds later.

"Yes," I sighed in relief. I put them on and sighed again when everything came into focus. I peered at the screen. The image was grainy and in black and white, but he did look a lot like the guy I'd seen in the parking lot of the courthouse.

"He probably saw you leave with me," Cope muttered.

"What exactly happened over there?"

"He was looking for something and wasn't too happy when he couldn't find it." He turned the laptop back so he could study the image. "Any idea what it might've been?"

"None."

"Ali?"

"Yeah?"

"No idea?"

"Obviously, my laptop."

He leaned against the back of the stool. "Why, though? It doesn't make sense."

"Like you said, he probably saw me leave with you. Maybe he thought I knew something about Warrick's trial."

He nodded and continued studying the image. "It's plausible."

It wasn't and we both knew it. However, there was more than one reason I couldn't give him the answers he was looking for.

12

Cope

The entire drive from my apartment to the court-house in Virginia, the same thing rolled over in my mind. Ali had lied to me yesterday. She was hiding something, and it pissed me the fuck off. Stella's words echoed in my mind, and I couldn't help but wonder if I should call Decker and have him run a check on her.

She couldn't know the real story about Irish. Of that, I was certain. So what was it? What could someone have been looking for in her apartment? It would've made more sense if they'd broken into mine.

After Rock left, Ali and I had a quiet afternoon, the tension between us thick. She'd slept the majority of the day, which was the best thing for her.

I spent the time pouring through everything Deck had sent over on the most recent names I'd given him. Without my asking, he'd also been able to get into some of the agency's files I wouldn't have been able to access from home, as well as some I wouldn't have been able to access from anywhere. The man was fucking scary; now wasn't the first time I was damn glad we were on the same side.

I checked on Ali one more time after my mom arrived at the apartment and before I left for Virginia this morning, and she was still asleep. I longed to walk over to the bed and kiss her goodbye, but stopped myself. A wall had gone up between us yesterday after she hadn't been honest with me. I was sure she'd realized it as much as I had.

I'd just pulled into the parking garage when the cell rang with a call from my father.

"Good morning, Senator."

"Just checking in, son."

"I've just arrived at the district courthouse." I scrubbed my face with my hand. "Dad, when I can tell you something, I will. Please don't ask."

"I'm worried about you."

"I appreciate that, but I've got this under control."

"Your mother mentioned something about a reporter staying in your apartment."

Here it came. The line of questioning I'd expected from my mom was coming from him instead.

"I don't have time to get into it now, Dad."

"I don't need to tell you to watch your back with the media, Sumner."

"How's the reporter?" asked Hammer when I walked into the courthouse and found him waiting.

"Fine."

Hammer leaned closer. "Somethin' up your ass this mornin', Cope?"

Too many things, to be honest, but I wasn't about to tell Hammer that. "You ready?"

He shook his head, laughed, and stalked off in the direction of the meeting room, motioning for me to follow. "Showtime."

Warrick looked up when we walked in. "Everything okay, Cope?" he asked. "I heard there was an accident."

"Everything's fine."

I heard Hammer sneer, but I didn't have it in me. I knew I was supposed to act like Irish was pond scum, but was it really necessary? I was a CIA agent, trained to hide my feelings. It would be amateurish for me to act the same way Hammer was.

I caught a look that passed between Irish and his lead attorney. Damon Church was one of the top federal defense attorneys in the country—and had absolutely no idea the man he was currently representing didn't truly need his help. Unless what I had planned failed. If it did, he'd likely be my attorney too.

The man seated directly across from me cleared his throat and rested his arms on the table. "Mr. Warrick has requested a private conversation."

"With?"

"You."

I looked from Church to Irish and nodded once.

"Cope?" I heard Hammer say, but I didn't turn to look at him. I kept my eyes on Irish.

"Clear the room."

"Fuck," Hammer said under his breath and pushed his chair back. The rest of Irish's team walked out, leaving Hammer and Church. Both were doing their damnedest to be the one who closed the door behind them. I was beginning to think Hammer should consider a career in acting. Then again, acting is what made an agent.

"Wait," I called after them. "I want both of you to state, on the record, that there will be no surveillance whatsoever of the conversation Warrick and I are about to have."

Church grinned. "Why, Agent Copeland," he drawled, "that would be illegal, son."

"You both heard me."

"No surveillance," said Hammer, taking a step closer to Church, a man close to a foot shorter than him and weighing in a good fifty pounds less, not that he backed away.

"No surveillance," he said, motioning for Hammer to leave the room first.

Hammer bowed. "After you."

"Get the fuck out of here!" I yelled at the two of them. I settled my gaze back on Irish.

"How are you holding up?" I asked once I made sure the door was closed.

"I've been in worse situations."

His positive attitude surprised me.

"Just tell me you're getting somewhere while I'm sitting in jail with my thumb in my ass."

"I am."

He scrubbed his face with his hand. "Until we can wrap this up, there are still agents at risk, Cope."

"I know that, Irish." Once again, I hated that no one knew this man the way I did. The majority of people believed him to be a traitor, and he was as far from it as he could get.

"I dropped the bait; I'm just waiting to see who bites."

He nodded.

"We need to talk about what's going to happen when this is over."

His eyes met mine. "What do you mean?"

"I'm not going back."

"Back?"

"I took leave. Listen, Irish, the woman who was hit was driving my car—that was no accident. It was done intentionally."

"Hammer told me."

"Decker's adding another couple of men on the inside with you and Rage."

Irish nodded again. "Who?"

I told him I'd leave that decision to Deck.

"So you said you've been thinking about what's going to happen when this is over."

"That's right."

"And you're not going back to the agency. What are you going to do?"

"I'm thinking about joining up with the Invincibles."

"They all despise me."

"They don't have any idea who you really are, Irish."

When I returned to the apartment, my mother was in the kitchen, preparing lunch. Ali sat at the counter, setting up her new laptop.

"You're back early," said my mom, looking at her watch.

I nodded but had no intention of commenting on why to either of them. At least not until my mother left. I owed Ali a briefing, and I'd deliver.

"Sumner, are you all right?"

"Of course, Mom."

"You seem particularly tense." She looked at Ali. "Not that he isn't always."

Ali turned to me, cocked her head, and smiled.

"You're welcome to head home now…I mean, if you have things to do." My mother looked surprised and maybe hurt, but I was trying to be nice, considering I'd asked her to be here every day this week.

"You don't have to go into the office?"

"No."

"Very well, then," she said, wiping her hands on a towel. "I'll just leave this in the refrigerator for when Ali is ready."

The woman seated at my kitchen counter turned her head toward me and smirked. Yes, I had caught her mention that the food wasn't for me.

I walked my mother to the door. "She's lovely, Sumner."

I nodded and kissed my mother's cheek. That Ali was lovely—gorgeous really, not to mention hot as fuck—wasn't something that needed to be pointed out to me.

"You've a fan in my mother," I told her, pulling out the stool next to her.

"The feeling is mutual."

She said the words, but there was no feeling behind them. Even her eyes were hooded.

"Did everything go okay while I was gone?"

Her eyes scrunched. "Yes."

"I owe you a story."

She didn't say anything. In fact, she turned her head away.

"Ali? Would you rather wait until later?"

"What I'd really like to do is go back to my apartment."

Even when she was angry with me—on the countless occasions she had been, in the short time we'd known each other—her mood hadn't seemed as off as it did now. It had begun yesterday, when she lied, but that didn't explain why she was mad at *me*. It should be the other way around.

"Let me make a call." I stood and walked into the bedroom, where I saw her belongings were all packed in the bag I'd brought over for her.

"Ali wants to go back to the apartment," I said when Rock answered. "Any issue with that?"

"None."

"You're sure?"

"You want me to invent one?"

I didn't like the idea of her being over there alone, but that wasn't the real issue. I wanted her here with me. Even if things were tentative between us, at least I could be near her. And how fucked up was that?

I was sitting on the bed, still staring at my phone after I ended my call with Rock, when I heard her say, "Hey," from the doorway. I looked up.

"Hey."

"I'm sorry, Cope. I'm not used to having to rely on someone twenty-four hours a day. I've been on my own a really long time."

"You don't have to explain."

She came over and sat beside me. "I feel like I should." She took a deep breath. "My dad died when I was sixteen. Less than a year later, my mom suffered an aneurysm and died too."

"That must've been really hard on you."

She looked down at the floor. "It isn't something I talk about very often."

"You don't have to now."

She got up and went around the end of the bed to the other side. When she stretched out on it, I did the same, as though our lying side by side was the most natural thing in the world.

"My dad was in construction. Mainly commercial. The town I'm from is old, which means when property is renovated, they often find asbestos. They eventually realized it could cause cancer, but that was years after my father began working. He died of lung cancer."

"I'm sorry, Ali."

"It was really hard on my mom, as you can imagine. Especially since she had to fight to get the company he'd worked for to pay for his medical expenses. In the end, they settled with her, and she got a large payout from them, not just for the bills, but for wrongful death. It took a lot out of her."

"You said she had an aneurysm?"

"I was sitting in the kitchen, talking to her. She opened the refrigerator door and then…dropped to the floor."

I turned on my side so I could look at her; she was staring at the ceiling.

"I don't know what I would've done without Chloe. She was…so supportive."

"I'm glad you had her in your life."

She turned her head and looked at me. "You're a nice guy, Cope."

I brought my hand to my heart. "Always the nice guy. They finish last, you know."

Ali looked back up at the ceiling. "I'm not used to being around people."

"Me either, to tell you the truth." I couldn't stand it anymore. I had to ask. "Ali?"

"Yeah?"

"Are you sure you have no idea what someone might've been looking for the other night?"

"I already said I didn't," she answered too quickly.

Fuck, she just lied again.

I sat up and turned so my back was to her. "Rock said they're done over at your apartment. You can go back whenever you're ready."

13

Ali

Cope stood and walked out of the room; he knew I was lying. Although it was more complicated than the question he'd asked me.

Earlier, while his mother made my lunch, I received an email from Jessica, saying Money wanted to meet. With Cope or his mother watching me every minute of the day and night, I had no idea how I was going to manage getting away.

I eased off the bed, wheeled my suitcase out, but didn't see Cope anywhere. The apartment wasn't that big and the bathroom door was open, so I knew he wasn't in there. As odd as it was, I could only assume he'd left. I tore a piece of paper from the pad near the refrigerator and started to write him a note.

What would I say? *Hey, thanks for everything. You know, staying with me in the hospital, bringing me into your home, caring for me.*

I eased myself onto the stool by the bar and opened my laptop. I'd wait to leave until Cope came back, so I could thank him in person.

Three hours later, I eased back off the stool I'd been sitting on for so long, I was stiff. Since Cope hadn't bothered to tell me he was leaving, I didn't bother either.

"Who are you?" I asked the man perched outside the door of my apartment.

"Name's Buck, ma'am," he said, holding his hand out to shake mine. "Can I help you with your bags?"

"I'm good. Thanks." I put my card in the reader, and he opened the door for me.

"Who do you work for, Buck?" I asked over my shoulder, holding the door open with my leg.

"I'm a private contractor, ma'am."

Not an answer, but obviously, he worked for the agency. "Is Buck your real name?"

He shook his head. "No, ma'am."

"I'm going to ask you one more question, and this time, I want you to answer it."

He nodded his head once.

"How old are you?"

"I'm thirty, ma'am."

"That's what I thought. I'm two years younger than you are, Buck, so I'd appreciate it if you stopped calling me ma'am." I let the door close without waiting for a response.

Once inside, I left my bags near the door and rummaged through my purse, looking for my pain pills. Stupidly, I hadn't taken one earlier, figuring I would in a few minutes once I got over here. Instead, I'd sat in Cope's apartment for three hours. My body ached, and all I wanted to do was lie down on the bed and sleep until the pain went away.

I took two instead of the one recommended and went into the bedroom, feeling even more stupid when I found myself wishing Cope was with me.

When I woke, it was dark outside. I gingerly rolled and eased myself off the mattress. Time for another pain pill, followed by more sleep. After deciding I'd better take only one this time, I finished the water I'd poured into a glass and walked as close to the windows as I was comfortable.

From there, it didn't appear there were any lights on in Cope's place. I took two more cautious steps forward and peeked around the corner. The draperies were open, and the apartment looked completely dark. I was about to take a step backward when something near Cope's window caught my eye. Light reflected off a glass held by the silhouette of a man as he raised it in my direction. Why was he sitting over there in the dark? Was he angry I left without so much as a thank you?

I raised my hand but couldn't see if the silhouette moved.

After a couple of minutes, I went back into the bedroom where I'd left my phone and called him. When it only rang twice before going to voicemail, I pressed end without leaving a message.

14

Cope

Ali didn't owe me a damn thing, I decided while I sat on a bench outside the Civil War Museum. Whatever was bothering her was none of my business—even if she had lied to me.

The minute I found out she was a reporter, I knew I had to stay away from her, but I'd ignored my own warning and got as close to her as I could.

If she hadn't been in an accident and broken her arm, she probably wouldn't have been in my bed—where I'd almost sunk my cock into her wet heat. The fear that I'd hurt her had been the only thing stopping me from doing it, and my body still ached from that decision. Her lying, something that would normally be a deal breaker for me, hadn't done anything to ease my raging desire to fuck her into next week.

After ten minutes of forcing myself not to think about her, I was able to get up and walk to my rental car without the tent in my pants embarrassing me. I drove back to DC without feeling the slightest bit better than when I'd left.

My cell vibrated at the same time the number of the caller flashed on the screen. I hit the call button on my steering wheel. "Cope," I answered.

"She just left," said Rock.

"Copy that."

A few minutes later, another call came in from a different number. "Hey, Cope, it's Buck. Thalia's landed."

"Copy that," I muttered a second time before ending the call. Ali, or Thalia, as the team had begun referring to her at my request, was back at her apartment.

I was surprised she'd waited so long to leave my place, but now that she was gone, I could go home.

I didn't bother turning on the lights when I walked into my loft. I had no desire to see its emptiness. I breathed in deeply; Ali's scent still wafted in the air. Soon enough, it would be gone, but I doubted the memory of her body in my bed would fade as quickly.

I poured myself a drink, ignoring the call coming in from my father, appreciating his concern, but like every other time he'd asked, there was nothing I could tell him. I powered the phone off, walked to the window, and looked over at Ali's dark apartment, wishing that instead of sleeping there, she was still here.

As I stood in the shadows, I saw the light come on and took a sip of the bourbon in my glass. When the light flickered, I took another step back. I held my breath, wondering if she would be brave enough to step closer to look for me.

She stared openly, turning her head. I raised my glass. Windows and a few hundred feet separated us, and yet I could swear I heard her gasp when she caught the light's reflection on the ice. She looked right at me and raised her hand. I took another drink.

Did she know that from here I could see the outline of her body under her sheer robe? Was she aware I could see when she brought her thighs together, perhaps remembering how I'd kissed the inside of them?

How I'd wanted to run my tongue up until I reached her panties, so wet with need. I took another sip, breathing in the bite of the bourbon when in my mind, it was her scent that lingered.

She reached out for the brick of the wall and slowly took a step back. I stayed where I was, my glass empty, until the lights went out.

I stretched my neck, looking up at the high ceiling of my apartment. I needed another fucking drink. Anything that would help me forget her ocean eyes.

On my way to the kitchen, I reached over my shoulder, grabbed my shirt, and pulled it over my head, tossing it on the floor. After unfastening my belt, I pulled it through the loops and threw it against the wall.

I shuddered, overcome by the memory of the way her breath had hitched when I brought my mouth to her nipple. I dropped three ice cubes into the glass and watched as they steamed when the amber liquid slid over their hard edges.

I pulled at the buttons on my jeans, about to drop them where I stood, when I heard a knock at the door. "What the fuck?" I muttered and then remembered I'd turned my phone off. I had all but the top button refastened when I threw the door open without looking to see who was on the other side.

"Um…hi." Ali's eyes traveled from my face down my body. When I saw Rock and Buck standing a few feet away, I pulled her into my dark apartment.

"What are you doing here?" I asked, fumbling for the light switch.

4:44 she WHISPERED. "Leave it off," she whispered, resting her right hand on the waist of my jeans.

"Ali—" I groaned when her fingertips slipped inside the open v of my jeans.

"I'm sorry," she murmured.

I put my hand on hers, stopping her fingers from going any lower. "What for?"

"Leaving…" I felt her lips on my sternum. "Without thanking you."

I reached for the switch and flicked it on, flooding the space with bright light.

Ali took a step back and lowered her gaze to the floor. "I saw you…were back."

"I'm sorry I left."

She looked into my eyes. "Why did you?"

Why had I? Because I couldn't stand the thought of her leaving and being in my apartment without her any more than I could stand that she'd lied to me.

"Cope?" she whispered.

I shook my head, laughed, and took a step closer to her. "You're going to think I've lost my mind," I mumbled, angling my head and leaning down so my lips were close enough to touch hers.

"Tell me."

"I hated the idea…"

Her breath hitched just like it had when I circled her nipple with my tongue, and I kissed her. Bracing my body so I didn't lean into hers, I held her face with my other hand and kissed her harder. I stopped and rested my forehead against hers. "I'm so afraid I'm going to hurt you."

She tried to turn her head away. "I shouldn't have come back."

"Is that what I said?"

"No, but…"

"I didn't want you to leave in the first place."

"It seemed like you did."

"Come on," I said, taking her hand and leading her farther inside. I stopped when I reached the hallway, and Ali dropped my hand.

"Do you want to have a seat?" I motioned with my head to the sofa.

She shook her head.

"In there?" I asked, motioning to the bedroom.

"Please."

She wore my sweatshirt that was three sizes too big for her. I stood behind her and grasped the hem, slowly bringing it up. She slipped her right arm out of it, and I pulled it over her head. She wiggled her left arm until the garment fell to the floor. I reached around her body and covered her breasts with both of my hands. I kissed her neck, her shoulder, the side of her face. "Get on the bed, Ali."

She turned around and used the fingers of one hand to pull off her yoga pants and the black lace panties that matched the bra I'd told her not to wear earlier. I picked them up, needing to know how wet they were.

Ali took my other hand and brought it between her legs. I dragged my finger through her folds. "You still aren't on the bed, baby."

She scooted back, sat, and spread her legs. I went on my knees between them and buried my face in her pussy. When she fell back on the bed, I reached up with both my hands and pinched her nipples as I tortured her clit with the tip of my tongue. I peeked up at the woman writhing on my bed and looking down at me.

"Cope," she whispered. "Please."

"Please what, Ali? Tell me what you need."

"Fuck me."

I stood, pulled open the buttons on my jeans, and let them drop to the floor. "Put your legs around my waist."

When she did, I raised her torso and rested my cock against her entrance. "If I do anything to hurt you…"

She smiled and bucked her hips. I pushed into her and stopped.

When she groaned my name, I thrust a little deeper. I kept my hands on her body and moved her hips against me.

Ali's head rocked from side to side, and she threw her arms above it. I saw what she was about to do, but not in time to stop her.

"Ouch," she groaned when she hit herself in the head with her cast. I held her still, my cock pulsing inside her, wondering if the moment was ruined. "Sexiest thing ever, right?" she said with a grin.

I took a deep breath, pulling her hips toward me while my eyes trailed her body. "There's no one sexier, Ali," I murmured, wishing I could take her hard, but still so afraid of hurting her. Just the idea that I was inside her warm wetness nearly had me ready to lose it. Instead, I focused on her, spreading her open with my fingers so I could pinch her clit while I eased in and out.

"Oh, God," she groaned, trying to move against me, but I kept her still with the hand still on her hip.

"Not so fast, baby."

"I need it fast," she whined. "Fast and hard."

"We'll get there." I rolled my hips and pulled out, falling again to my knees. Pinching her clit between two fingers, I thrust two from my other hand into her warm channel and curled them toward me. "Come on, baby. Let me see how you look when you fall apart." Moments later, she cried out, her head thrashing from side to side. I looked down at my unsheathed cock, realizing how close I'd been to coming inside her.

"Get all the way up on the bed, baby," I said, gingerly helping her move.

"Cope?" she called out when I walked into the bathroom.

"Almost forgot this," I said, holding up a foil packet when I came back to lie beside her.

Ali's eyes were wide as I rolled the condom on my length. I grabbed a pillow, put it under her hips, and spread her legs open. I eased back into her and held her hips like I had before.

"I want you to be still. Lie there and take all the pleasure I have to give you."

Ali groaned and arched her neck when I thrust into her again and again.

"Look at me," I demanded when I knew I wouldn't last any longer. I came, staring into Ali's ocean eyes, wondering if she had any idea how much she'd come to mean to me in such a short amount of time.

15

Ali

I was sore. So sore. Every inch of my body ached when I opened my eyes and saw the sun was shining. It was dawn when we finally gave in to sleep.

Cope had rolled me to my side and nestled my back to his front. "Sleep, baby," he'd murmured.

I eased from the bed and pulled his sweatshirt over my head, not bothering to try to get my left arm into the sleeve. Since it came down to my knees, I didn't bother with panties either.

After using the restroom, I walked down the hall-way to the kitchen, realizing almost too late that Cope, who'd told me he had to go into the office today, would be gone by now and his mother would be here in his place. Instead, the apartment appeared empty.

"Hello?" I called out, but got no answer. I saw what looked like a note propped up against the espresso machine.

Good morning, baby. When you read this, first send me a photo of your beautiful face. Second, call the café, and Lindsey will bring you coffee and breakfast.

I mussed my hair and let it drape over one side of my face, bit my bottom lip, and sent it to Cope before I could talk myself out of it. I'd just set my phone on the counter when it vibrated with a one-word response. *Fuck.* I laughed and turned on the espresso maker. I'd figured out the one in my apartment; I was sure I could figure out this one too.

I sat on a stool and was about to look for an instructional video when I heard the front door lock click.

"Ali, good morning," said Cope's mother, walking in, followed by Buck, carrying bags of groceries. "I'm sorry I'm so late. I had to stop by the market and pick up a few things. Sumner doesn't keep much food in the apartment."

"I'll be back," said Buck after setting the bags on the counter. I bit my tongue from asking if there were more groceries. A few minutes later, he came back, carrying several more bags.

"Is there more?" I mouthed when Mrs. Copeland turned her back.

Buck shook his head. "Is there anything else, ma'am?" he asked, pointing to Cope's mom. I chuckled, remembering how I'd asked him to stop calling me ma'am.

I got the impression that Buck, with his scruffy beard and dancing eyes filled with a spark of mischief, would be a lot of fun to hang out with. He was way more my speed than the buttoned-up *Sumner.* But damn, if that man hadn't gotten under my skin and into my panties.

When Mrs. Copeland finally told Buck "that would be all," he tipped his hat and walked out.

"I didn't realize they let agents wear cowboy hats to work these days," she muttered under her breath.

"I feel like this has been a big inconvenience for you for nothing."

"What do you mean?"

"I told Cope, err, Sumner, that I'd be going back to my apartment this morning. I'm sorry for our lack of communication."

I saw her son's face in how she studied me. They had the same green eyes. "I'm surprised he didn't mention it to me."

"As I said, I apologize—"

She took out her phone, tapped the screen, and brought it to her ear. She drummed her fingernails on the counter and then tapped the screen again. "You don't mind waiting until my son responds, do you?"

Of course I fucking mind waiting until your son responds, I shouted inside my head. "With all due respect, Mrs. Copeland—"

"Call me Laurel."

"With all due respect, Laurel, I do mind. It was kind of your son to offer to let me stay here, but it isn't necessary I do so any longer. I appreciate all you've done for me as well."

It occurred to me that in order for me to have a dramatic exit, I was going to have to climb off this stool, go into the bedroom, put my pants—and panties—on, and leave. *Laurel* would likely ask if I needed help with my bag, at which point I'd have to tell her it was already at my apartment. *Gawd.*

"You know what? Instead, I think I'll just go take a pain pill and lie down. You wouldn't mind, would you, Laurel?"

"Of course I wouldn't, dear. Make yourself right at home."

I smiled and slid off the stool, wishing she'd turn around so I could do my walk of shame back to Cope's bedroom without her witnessing it. Instead, I could feel her eyes on me every damn step of the way.

I was lying on the bed, bored out of my mind, cursing myself for not having the balls to just leave, when my cell rang.

"Hey," I answered.

"I have two things to say and am not sure how much longer I'll be alone. So here goes: first, that photo you sent—*Jesus*—you looked hot. I've never wanted to own a helicopter more in my life."

"A helicopter?"

"So I don't have to endure the painful drive back to you while trying to stop myself from looking at it again."

I giggled. "What was the second thing?"

"I'm sorry about my mom."

"Don't be. If I hadn't slept so late, I would've been long gone by the time she got here."

"That's my fault too. I didn't let you get much sleep. Where are you now?"

"Same place I was last night."

"I wish I was there," he murmured so quietly I could barely hear him.

"One of us has to get some work done."

"Speaking of work. I'm ready whenever you are."

I looked up at the ceiling, wondering if I should just tell Cope to forget it, but that might make him more suspicious than my lying to him had.

"Ali?"

"I'm here."

"Hammer is headed back into my office, so I better end this call. Will you still be there when I get home?" It sounded like Cope's hand went over the phone's mic. In the background, I could hear muffled voices. "I'll see you later, baby."

His voice was so sexy, I wanted to crawl through the now-ended call and wrap my legs around his waist. I rolled over on my side and dropped my phone on the bed. What was wrong with me? Since when was I sex-starved-Suzy?

I'd had boyfriends…and sex. It had been okay. I mean, sometimes it was better than okay, but it had never been great…until last night. Sex with Cope was off-the-fucking-charts great. And I couldn't let it happen again.

Again, what had I been thinking? I'd been hired to find out whether Sumner Copeland was as dirty of an agent as Paxon Warrick. I had no doubt many approached similar assignments by having sex with the person they were investigating, but that wasn't who I was. At least not who I was before I met Cope.

Rolling from the bed, I grabbed the clothes that would cover the bottom half of my body, pulled them on as best I could with the use of only one arm, and gathered my dignity.

"How was your nap, dear?" asked Laurel when I walked down the hallway and found her sitting on the sofa, reading.

"Great, thanks. I'm…um…I need my…uh…laptop."

She set her book down. "Before you go, I was wondering if you and I might have a chat?"

"It isn't the best time. I have—"

She stood. "Ali, please?"

I walked over and was about to sit in the chair when she sat back down and patted the sofa beside her. I swallowed my groan and did her bidding. "What do you want to chat about?"

She weaved her fingers together and rested her hands on her knee. "I can't help but notice that my son is quite taken with you."

"Your son doesn't know me, Mrs. Copeland."

She raised a brow, and I didn't care. Before she could say anything else, I stood. "Sumner and I met less than a week ago when I arrived in town to cover the trial of Paxon Warrick on behalf of the *Express*. After a handful of serendipitous encounters, during which your son portrayed a side of himself I have since learned isn't typical of him, he felt obligated to look out for me. I am a journalist, your son is a handler for the CIA, and you are the wife of a senator who believes that people like me are his worst enemy, likely rightly so.

"Please do not misunderstand me. I appreciate everything you and your son have done for me. However, we both know that it doesn't matter whether Sumner is taken with me or not. Goodbye, Mrs. Copeland."

I squared my shoulders and walked to the door of the apartment.

"You're wrong," I heard her say from behind me.

I stopped and looked up at the ceiling, knowing my mother would be ashamed of me if I walked out without responding. I turned around, and she was within a foot of me. "Mrs. Copeland—"

She held up a hand. "I, too, am quite taken with you, Ali. In many ways, you remind me of myself. What I was going to say, had you let me finish, is that I hope neither Sumner nor I have reason to regret it."

There was nothing more for me to add. She would. And so would her son.

I was just inside my apartment when my cell rang with a call from Jessica.

"I'm sorry I didn't call you. Cope—"

"It's okay, but listen. Something else has gone down, I'm not sure what or with whom, but Money is looking into it. He wants to hold off on meeting until next week, when he knows what it is."

I ended the call, silently praying that whatever had gone down wasn't something that would further implicate Cope. I shook my head, knowing what I really should do was call Jessica back and tell her to assign someone else to this investigation. Instead, I opened a bottle of wine.

16

Cope

When I got out of the elevator, Buck stood and walked toward me.

"Ali asked me to give you this." He handed me an envelope. I took a step forward, and he moved between me and Ali's door and shook his head. "She doesn't want to see you, Cope."

"Is that right?"

Buck nodded. "Read it."

"You know what's in it?" I asked, when what I really wanted to do was tell the asshole to fuck off.

"You know better than that."

"What's going on here, Buck?"

He took off his cowboy hat and ran his hand through his long hair.

"You need to see a barber."

His eyes opened wide, and he laughed. "Probably right." The smile left his face. "I'm not exactly sure what set it off, but if I had to guess, I'd say your mother and Ali may have had words."

He had to be wrong. That didn't sound like either of them. "What happened?"

"About two hours after your mother showed up at your apartment with a month's worth of groceries, Ali stormed out of it. She didn't say anything until after we were off the elevator and headed over to her building."

"Who was?"

"Ali and me."

"Go on."

"She's usually pretty friendly, but not today. At least not then. She stopped at the entrance to the building and asked me not to come upstairs."

"You went anyway?"

"Of course I did. As I told her, it was the job I was hired to do."

"Then what?"

Buck laughed. "She tried mighty hard to slam the door. I think she might've hurt herself doin' it."

Before I could react to Ali being hurt, her door swung open. She stood on the threshold with her right hand on her hip. "I can hear you talking about me."

"Have I told any lies?" Buck asked her in a tone that was far too flirtatious in my opinion. Where in the hell was Rock, anyway?

"You're here. You might as well come in." She waved her hand at me and glared at Buck, who just kept laughing.

I followed her into the kitchen.

"Can I get you anything?" she asked.

I nodded at the half-full bottle of wine on the counter. "Are you supposed to be drinking that while you're on pain meds?"

"Do you want a glass or not?"

"Sure." I pulled out a stool at the kitchen counter and sat. "What's this all about, Ali?" I asked, waving the envelope.

"It's a thank you note." She set a glass of wine in front of me and turned to look in the refrigerator. "I'd offer you something to eat, but I haven't had a chance to go to the market."

"What happened between you and my mom?"

"We had a friendly conversation, during which she warned me away from you, and I listened."

It was all I could do not to let my jaw drop. "You're kidding."

She took a hefty swig of the wine in her glass and refilled it with what was left in the bottle. "That was the gist of it."

I stood, walked around the counter, took Ali's glass from her hand, and set it down. She ran her hand through her hair, like Buck had, only she dragged it over her face. "How much of this have you had?" I asked when I opened the trash to throw the one away and saw a second empty bottle.

"I didn't drink all of that one."

I wanted to ask who had and what she meant by "all," but that wasn't important—for now. She walked over to the sofa, plopped down on it in a way that led me to think she was feeling no pain, and rested her head against the back of it.

"This was a mistake," she said, staring up at the ceiling through the hair that covered most of her face.

"What exactly?"

"This. You. Especially you." She sat up and tried to fold her arms, and then evidently remembered one was in a cast. "Buck wasn't supposed to let you in."

I smiled and ran my finger down her cheek. "You let me in, Ali."

She flopped against the back of the couch again and closed her eyes. I moved the hair from her forehead.

"It's hopeless."

I shifted closer and put my arm around her. "Nothing's hopeless."

"It is. No matter how many times you move it, my hair just goes right back." She leaned over and rested her head on my shoulder.

"What happened today, Ali?"

She took a deep breath and blew it out, confirming she'd had at least some of the other bottle of wine. "She said you were taken with me, and she told me not to regret it. Wait. That isn't right. She told me not to make *you* regret it."

This was sounding more like my mother, but not quite. Something else must've happened. Rather than question Ali further, I'd ask my mom tomorrow.

"You will," she whispered.

"Not a chance."

"Why are you so nice to me?" She turned her body more and buried her head in my shoulder. Not five minutes later, when I heard her soft snores, I gathered her in my arms and carried her into the bedroom.

Her bed was already unmade, so I set her down and covered her with the sheet and blanket before toeing off my shoes, removing my tie and shirt, and dropping my pants. Ali's back was to me, so I curled myself around her body and draped my arm over her waist.

"I really like you, Cope."

"I really like you too, Ali."

I don't know how long it was before she got up and went into the bathroom. When she came back, she had taken off my sweatshirt and sat on the side of the bed. I got out on the other side, came around, and helped her remove her yoga pants.

"What about these?" she asked when I left her panties on. I removed those as carefully as I had her pants.

I was told what a good guy I was countless times in my life, to the point that I hated hearing it. Right now, I hated being it.

By the time I walked around the end of the bed and crawled in beside her, Ali was snoring again. Like before, I curled my body into hers and fell asleep too.

"Cope," Ali said, shaking me.

I opened my eyes. "What? Are you okay?"

"You have to go."

It took me a minute to figure out where I was. "What time is it?"

"Five. You have to go, or you'll be late."

I rested my head against the pillow. "It's Sunday, Ali, and even if it weren't, there'd be no court today."

"Why not?"

I hadn't made up my mind whether I'd tell her what happened, and she obviously hadn't heard. "Get back in bed." When she did, I drew her close to me. "They found a bomb in the courthouse Friday afternoon."

"What?"

When she tried to scoot away, I held her tighter.

"No one was hurt, and the bomb was diffused, but it means a continuance."

She wiggled free enough to raise her head and look at me. "You could've been killed."

So could've she, had she been there. For the first time since it happened, I was thankful for Ali's accident.

"I'm taking a leave from the agency."

"Why? Because of the bomb?"

"In part, but it isn't that simple. It's just a good idea until I get through this thing with Warrick. I'm distracted, and that isn't fair to the other agents I handle."

"What happens now?"

"We go back to sleep." I moved the sheet so I could see her breast, reached forward, and cupped it. "Unless you have a better idea."

"I'm serious."

I looked into her ocean eyes. "So am I," I said, moving my hand to cup her chin instead of her breast, and kissed her. I deepened it and moved my body over hers. When Ali reached for me, I covered her hand with mine. "Wait, baby."

Her eyes closed to slits and then reopened. "Why?"

"I don't have a condom."

She smiled and rolled away from me. "No promises." She opened the drawer of the nightstand. "Who knows how long they've been in here." She tossed a handful over her shoulder and turned on the light.

"They have a couple good years left in them," I told her, ripping a packet open with my teeth.

"Do you need help?" I asked later when I saw Ali staring at the coffeemaker.

"I know how to do it, it just takes more than one hand."

I came up behind her and reached under her arms. "Put them where you want them." I laughed when Ali placed my left hand on one of the dials and my right on her breast.

She adjusted something on the machine with her right hand, and steaming coffee flowed into the cup. She moved that one out of the way and grabbed another.

"You can move it, you know."

"Move what?"

"Your hand."

I let go of the knob.

"Not that one," she said, placing it back where it was.

"This one?" I squeezed her tit.

"Move it more."

I trailed it down her body and between her legs. "Is this better?"

"Much," she groaned, leaning against me while the machine filled the second cup of coffee.

When I thrust two fingers inside her and rubbed her clit with the pad of my thumb, Ali cried out. "God, Cope." She writhed, rubbing her ass against my cock until I thought I'd come too. She cried out once more and dropped her head. If my hand weren't still between her legs, she might've sunk to the floor. I lifted her in my arms and carried her back to the bed.

"But…coffee!" she cried.

I leaned down and kissed her. "Be right back."

I'd just poured cream into Ali's cup when I heard my phone ringing in the bedroom. Given the time, I had it set to do-not-disturb mode. There were only two types of calls that rang through. It was either one of my parents or a call being forwarded from my secure unit.

I set Ali's cup on the bedside stand beside her. "That's hot," I told her and laughed when she rolled her eyes.

"You're such a Boy Scout."

I grabbed my phone and went back to the kitchen to get my coffee, disturbed to see that the call I'd missed was from my dad.

If I had a stitch of clothing on, I would've gone outside the apartment door to return his call, but given Rock was out there, I'd spare him.

"Everything okay?" I asked when my father answered.

"What happened Friday?"

"Haven't you received the brief?"

"Sumner, I insist you tell me what you've gotten yourself mixed up in. Whatever it is, I'll help you in any way I can."

"Dad, I need you to trust that I know what I'm doing. If a time comes when I need your help, I'll let you know."

"I love you, son."

I ended the call and took a sip of my coffee. When I returned to the bedroom, Ali was staring into space.

"Are you okay?" I asked her.

"Are you?"

"My dad," I answered, shaking my head.

"You shouldn't talk to me about him."

I set my coffee down and got back into bed. "Because of what happened yesterday with my mom?"

"Because I'm a journalist."

"You're right."

"You shouldn't talk to me at all."

I rolled to my side and studied her. "Ali?"

She looked from the blank wall to me. "I'm serious, Cope."

"I've been down this road a time or two. I know what I can talk about and what I can't."

"This is why we shouldn't see each other anymore." She waved her hand over the bed. "Like this."

"I didn't handle our conversation very well that day when I drove you back from the courthouse and I said that because you were a reporter, we shouldn't talk. I didn't handle much of anything well that day but, Ali, I believe we're both adult enough to know which lines not to cross."

"Are we? Because I'd say we crossed the biggest of them all."

I lay on my back and looked up at the ceiling. I understood what she was saying. She was right, and I didn't want to accept it.

"What about your job?"

"I'm sure I'll be assigned to something else."

"Ali?"

"What?"

"What's going on?"

"What do you mean?"

"What else will you be assigned to?"

"I don't know." She shrugged and looked to her left.

It was a slight tell, but I was trained to recognize it. Ali fucking lied to me—again. I felt the muscles in my shoulders tense, and I was about to get out of bed and storm back to my apartment. But was that who I was? I didn't walk away when someone lied to me. I called them out on it.

"Let's try that again, but with the truth this time."

Instead of me getting out of bed and storming off, Ali did. She went into the bathroom and closed the door. Maybe she expected that when she came out, I'd be gone, but I wouldn't be. As crazy as it was, I cared about Ali Graham. I wanted this thing between us to work, and that meant, instead of lying, we needed to handle what we could and couldn't tell each other differently.

When I heard water come on, I got out of bed and walked over to the bathroom door, relieved to find she hadn't locked it. When I opened it, she was getting into the tub. Since I was already naked, I walked over and climbed in too. I didn't sit behind her; we were going to face each other and have this conversation.

17

Ali

Cope wrapped his hand around my ankle and brought my foot to the middle of his chest. I loved seeing his hands on me. Feeling them too. I didn't like him crawling inside of my head, though. I closed my eyes and focused on his fingers digging into the arch of my foot.

The worst part was, if I told Jessica I felt like I was in over my head with him, she'd encourage me to keep going.

"Ali," I heard him murmur.

I tried to wrench my foot away, but he held on. "I'm not letting go."

"Even if I drown?"

"Especially if you do."

I opened my eyes and studied him. "I can't talk to you about my work, Cope."

"There will be times I can't talk to you about mine either, but it isn't necessary to lie about it."

His fingertips trailed up the inside of my leg. "We can do this, Ali."

I closed my eyes and slid farther down into the tub, gasping when he thrust his fingers inside of me. I could hear him moving in the water, his other hand on my knee then on my hip. He grabbed my waist with both hands, set me on the edge of the tub, and spread my legs.

"Open your eyes and look at me."

I shook my head, refusing.

He brought his mouth to mine and kissed me. I wrapped my arm around his neck and, when he tried to pull back, held him tighter.

"You feel it too," he murmured.

I wanted to deny it. I couldn't. The attraction between us was more intense than anything I'd felt before. My eyes were still closed when he set me on my feet inside the tub, sat where I'd been sitting, and pulled my thighs so I straddled him.

"Come on, Ali," he growled. "Fuck me." I opened my eyes and saw he'd rolled on a condom. Positioning himself at my entrance, he eased me onto him. When I started to move, he wrapped his arms around my waist and held me still. Bending down, he sucked my nipple into his mouth.

"I need to move," I groaned.

"No."

I smiled. It wasn't just the sex. I really liked this guy. Too much. Way too much. Not just his mouth. Or his hands. Or the way his cock stretched and filled me. Him.

"Cope—"

He turned our bodies and stood. He was still inside me as he carried me to the bed. Our eyes met and I felt it. I was fucked, and not because he'd started moving inside me.

When I tried to get out of bed later, Cope snaked his arm around my waist and kissed my spine. I looked over my shoulder. "Aren't you hungry?"

"Always." He nibbled the soft skin of my waist, and I giggled. He let me go, rolled off the other side of the bed, and I watched him pick up his phone.

"Are you calling someone?"

"My mother."

I rolled my eyes and padded out to the kitchen. I was staring at my empty refrigerator when he joined me. "Get dressed, and we'll go over to my place."

I spun around. "Why?"

"Because I have food."

"I should stay here."

"Why?" He looked like a little boy who wasn't used to hearing no.

"I have work to do."

His nostrils flared, and he rubbed his hand through his hair. He turned and looked away from me. "I'll bring it back, then."

"What, food?" I laughed.

"You need to eat."

"I'll order something." Better yet, maybe once Cope left, I'd attempt going to the grocery.

He pulled out a stool and sat at the kitchen counter. I studied him. Something was on his mind.

"I feel like there's a lot you're not telling me, Ali."

I took a deep breath and turned away from him. "You're right. And there's a lot you're not telling me, Cope."

I heard the scrape of the stool on the tile floor and felt him walk closer. I closed my eyes, waiting for his touch.

"There's a difference between me not telling you something and you lying to me."

"That isn't fair."

"Isn't it?" he asked.

"Are you saying you haven't lied to me?"

"I haven't."

"Bullshit."

I knew when he walked away; I felt cold. I stayed where I was, looking at the windows I was too afraid to get closer to, until I heard him leave.

Once he was gone, I called Jessica, who told me the meeting with Money was still on hold. I assumed it was because of the bomb at the courthouse, and I was fine with that. I had nothing to tell him, and with Buck or Rock on constant vigil, I didn't know how I'd get away without one of them alerting Cope.

The division of the CIA I worked for was similar to the internal affairs department of other law enforcement agencies. When someone on the inside was suspected of operating outside their limits of power, agents like me were brought in. The nature of the investigations our department handled precluded other agents being alerted of our coming in, in fact, we reported to the Office of the Inspector General rather than the Director of the CIA. Keeping my identity a secret was also the reason I wasn't based in DC.

While I was good at my job, I wondered if the accident and the pain meds I was on because of it, were clouding my judgment.

I hadn't been on the case that long, but my gut was telling me Cope was clean. Like Money, the man who'd originally requested an internal affairs agent be assigned, I felt there was something about Cope's association with Irish that didn't make sense.

Money was looking for more than my gut instinct, though, which meant I had to figure out a way to get closer to Cope, and not just between the sheets.

Allowing him to leave earlier was a mistake that needed to be fixed.

18

Cope

A smart man would've walked out and kept going. Instead, I made it as far as the lobby of my building, turned around, and walked back across the street.

Rock was still on duty at Ali's apartment this morning, which meant he'd witnessed my indecision. As did the other two operatives Decker had brought in after her place was broken into.

"You okay, Cope?" Rock asked when I exited the elevator.

"No."

He smiled, but didn't comment further. With the mood I was in, if he had, he might've lost a few teeth.

I took a deep breath and knocked on the door. When Ali didn't answer after a couple of minutes, I took out my cell and called her. No answer to that either.

It was possible she was in the shower; it was also possible she had fallen or hurt herself or had a reaction to her medicine. I scrubbed my face with my hand. "I'm goin' in, Rock."

He handed me his key card, and I eased the door open. "Ali?" No answer. I let the door close behind me. "Ali, it's Cope. Where are you?" Still no answer. I rounded the corner into her bedroom and could hear her singing.

I smiled and opened the door to the bathroom. I didn't want to startle her. She was in the tub, eyes closed, with buds in her ears. I stood there for a minute, waiting for her to sense my presence, and began removing my clothes.

Once naked, I walked over to the tub, sat on the edge, leaned over, and kissed her shoulder. She opened her eyes and smiled but didn't give any indication that I'd surprised her.

"You knew I was here," I said when she removed one of the buds.

Her cheeks turned pink. "I wanted to see what you'd do."

"What if I'd left?"

"I would've called after you."

"Scoot forward." When she did, I climbed in behind her.

"I'm sorry about earlier, Cope."

"I am too."

"I understand there are things you can't discuss with me."

"I think we can make this work, Ali."

She sighed.

"You don't?"

"I don't know how long I'll be here."

"Why not? I would think the *Express* could keep you busy, especially with an election coming up." She was holding something back, but she'd been right earlier; I was holding something back too. In fact, the ramifications of what I couldn't tell her, had put her life in jeopardy.

"Can we agree, for now, not to talk about it?" she murmured.

I wrapped my arms around her waist. "Of course we can." I bent my neck and kissed the soft skin under her ear. She shuddered. "Ali…"

"What?"

"Is that short for anything?"

"No. My mother…her favorite movie was 'Love Story.'"

"I've never heard of it."

She laughed. "Ryan O'Neal and Ali McGraw fall in love, and she dies."

"Ah, so you were named after the character."

"No. The actress. The character's name was Jennifer, and my mom said there were a million girls my age with that name."

"Tell me more about them falling in love." I moved her hair and ran the tip of my tongue down her neck.

"It wasn't meant to be." She groaned when I reached up and pinched her nipple with my fingertips.

"Why not?"

"He was rich. She was poor."

"Was that all?" I cupped her mound with my other hand and slid one finger inside her.

"His family was powerful. They tried to break them up." Ali writhed against me.

"But he wouldn't stand for it."

She shook her head.

"How did she die?"

"Cancer."

"Tragic."

"It was a movie." She moved my hands and stood, holding hers out to me. I took it and stood too.

"I'm insatiable when it comes to you." I picked her up and climbed out of the tub, carrying her into the bedroom. I set her on the bed.

She wrapped both arms around me, resting her cast on my shoulder as I plowed into her warm wetness. I had to pull out, put on a condom, but wanted to feel her pussy clench my cock without any kind of barrier.

"Squeeze me." She did and I almost came. When I tried to pull out, Ali wrapped her legs around my waist. "I don't have a condom on, baby."

"I know."

Ali slept after I wrung her dry with pleasure. I stared up at the ceiling, stroking her hair with my fingers.

The last time Decker and I spoke, he asked if I wanted him to run a check on the reporter. I told him I already had. We both knew he could go deeper, and I didn't want him to. It was careless, but I wasn't ready to let her go. I might never be ready.

For the first time in many years, I'd started to see life beyond the mission Irish and I had taken on. Never had I dreamed it would go on as long as it had. Worse, the longer it did, the more agents we lost.

During the hotwash of one of our Chinese missions, Irish informed me his gut was telling him the targets knew their attackers were coming. While he'd made it out alive, three other agents hadn't. When it happened again a few months later, we both began paying closer attention.

The once-robust espionage network the agency had worked so hard to put in place in China, began falling apart. In the last five years alone, the loss of agents escalated at an alarming rate. Dozens of CIA informants had also disappeared—either jailed or killed.

When Irish came within an inch of losing his life a third time, we sat down in my apartment and, over a fifth of whiskey, reached an agreement.

"There's a mole," he'd said.

"Someone inside," I'd agreed.

"It's high up, Cope."

"I believe it is."

Even knowing it could end not only our careers but our lives, we made a pact to create a mission of our own. We took every Chinese op that presented itself, and began our investigation. In each one, Irish put himself at risk of death for the sole purpose of finding who was betraying our country, while I sat behind a desk. It ate at me to the point I'd suggested we give it up.

Irish had been livid with me and demanded I reconsider. It wasn't a week later that we were contacted by someone offering the information we were seeking.

The man, Dr. Benjamin, was a British diplomat and one of the world's leading experts on Chinese policy. Irish had been the one to appear on his radar, but he had enough evidence that we were on the right track, that we agreed to keep moving forward.

Within a week of our meeting, Benjamin, who had last been seen in Hong Kong, disappeared. Finding him became a mission we took on jointly with MI6.

Enter Decker Ashford and the Invincibles. MI6 had hired them to assist with the mission. It didn't take long before Deck came to me with the same suspicions Benjamin had about Irish. I'd had no choice at the time but to read him in.

The rest of the mission did not go in our favor. Irish became the lead suspect as the mole who was feeding information to Chinese intelligence officers.

We were at another crossroads when Decker suggested Irish take the fall, knowing we were close enough to finding the real mole that he'd be exonerated before he went to trial.

The result, though, was that when the wire services picked up the news that Warrick's case wouldn't be settled, reporters like Stella and Ali were assigned to cover it.

Stella had said there was something about Ali that didn't add up. I had to admit she didn't add up to me either. But I didn't care.

"What are you thinking about?" she murmured.

I turned my head and looked into her eyes. "You."

"Cope, I think we should—"

"No." I rolled to my side and grasped the back of her neck, pulling her close enough that I could capture her mouth with mine. This wasn't a kiss. I was claiming her.

19

Ali

"I got an email from my boss. She wants me to continue reporting on the trial," I told him the next morning.

"Okay," Cope said, looking up from where he stood in his kitchen, making scrambled eggs.

After another hours-long round of sex, we'd both agreed we needed to eat. Since I had no food and neither of us felt like going out, we went back to his apartment, ate, and then had more sex.

"What do you need from me?"

I wanted to say "nothing," but I still had a job to do. Even if I believed Cope was clean, I had to come up with enough evidence to prove it in order to complete my assignment.

It wouldn't be hard for me to attack it in the same way I would as an actual reporter; I did have a degree in journalism like the background check I was sure Cope had run, indicated. I'd double-majored with a degree in international studies, which is why the agency recruiter who'd visited Northwestern, approached me.

"I'll let you know."

"I think I can come up with something to make that easier." Cope pointed to my left hand when he noticed I was pecking at the keyboard with my index finger. He set a plate of eggs next to my laptop and then left the kitchen.

"You can eat first."

"Be right back," he hollered from the hallway.

Feeling as though I could think clearly for the first time since I got out of the hospital, I started an outline of the things that had happened since the trial began.

I thought back to the first day when Stella and I saw Cope storm out of the courtroom after only a little over an hour. That afternoon, someone had leaked a story about a deal. If that were a possibility, I would've received a brief about it from Money.

Next, was my accident, which had resulted in a continuance. The following night, my apartment had been broken into. I still hadn't come up with a reason for it. Cope had suggested that someone saw me with him, but the only thing that made sense was if someone was investigating me like I was him. Otherwise, there hadn't been enough time for my presence to raise any suspicion.

Cope didn't say anything about what had happened at the courthouse in the days between then and now, but I'd been checking the wires, and there were no reports on it, even from Stella.

Friday, someone had planted a bomb.

Cope walked up beside me and placed a rolled-up hand towel on the corner of my laptop, next to my keyboard. "See if this is the right height."

I rested my wrist on it.

"Can your fingers reach the keys?"

"Perfectly. Thank you, Cope."

He nodded and walked around the counter to get his plate. He came back and sat beside me. "Come up with anything yet?"

"Can you tell me more about the bomb?" I took a bite of my eggs.

He took a deep breath and let it out slowly before taking another bite of his food. This was something he didn't want to talk about.

"Where was it?"

"In the hallway behind the courtroom," he answered without looking at me.

"Behind the courtroom? Is that what you said?"

Cope nodded.

"There's no question, then, that the bomb was meant to go off during Warrick's trial?"

"That's right."

I rested against the back of the stool. "Cope?"

He set his fork down and turned his head slowly to look at me. "Yeah?"

"I was driving your car."

His eyes bored into mine as he watched me process through what he already knew. Someone was trying to kill him. Maybe Irish too, but definitely him.

I got up from the stool and paced.

"Ali?"

"Why you?" I asked, barely above a whisper.

His forehead was creased when he turned his head away.

"Cope? Why you?"

"I can't answer that."

"But you know the answer?"

"Ali, please."

"Fuck," I muttered under my breath. I needed to get out of here and think this through. I couldn't do it in front of him. I closed my laptop, unplugged it, and tucked it under my arm.

Maybe knowing there was nothing he could say to reassure me, Cope remained silent. Neither of us said another word when I walked out of his apartment.

"Want me to carry that for you?" Buck asked, pointing to my laptop.

I handed it to him without responding. My phone was in my pocket, but I'd left my bag and my key card behind.

"You can get into my apartment, right?"

He nodded.

As soon as the door closed behind me, I called Jessica.

"Someone is trying to kill Cope," I said before she could even say hello.

"Yes. That's one of the reasons Money wanted to wait to meet."

"I need a face-to-face now."

"Let me see what I can do."

I heard a knock at the door but knew it wasn't Cope. When I opened it, Rock handed me the bag I'd left in his apartment.

A few minutes later, Jessica called back. "I've been able to get a meeting set up in one hour at the *Express* offices."

I went into the bedroom and looked for something that might be easy for me to put on. I couldn't very well show up in Cope's sweatshirt that I'd been wearing for the last couple of days.

I managed to get into a pair of dress pants and a sweater, but didn't try to get my cast inside the left sleeve. The only thing I couldn't do a damned thing with was my hair. I looked out the peephole of the door, relieved to see that Buck was still out there, not Rock. He stood when I opened it.

"Hey, Miss Ali."

"Call me Ali."

He tipped his hat. "Anything you need?"

"As a matter of fact." I handed him my brush and dug a hair tie out of the pocket of my pants. "It looks like you might have some experience with this." I motioned to the ponytail hanging down his back.

"Turn around. Where you off to today?" he asked while he brushed my hair back and wrapped the tie around it.

"I have a meeting."

He handed me the brush. "Where?"

"Why?"

"I like to know where I'm goin'."

"Do you really have to go with me?" I asked even though I already knew the answer.

Buck nodded.

I turned to go back inside to grab my bag when something occurred to me. "Do you, uh, need to use the restroom or anything?"

"Thought you'd never ask."

I pointed toward the guest bath and went into the bedroom. When I came back out, Buck was waiting by the door.

"You must hate this part of the job."

He shrugged. "It could be worse. You're prettier than most of the people I have to keep my eye on."

I went back into the bedroom to grab a jacket. When I came back out, I didn't see Buck.

"Ready?" I asked when I found him perched outside my apartment door.

"Rock is downstairs, waiting with the car."

When we arrived at the *Express* building, Buck went in with me. I was about to sign him in as a visitor after I showed security my badge, but the man waved him through.

"Does he know you?" I asked as he led me over to the bank of elevators.

"Yes."

I shook my head at his abrupt response. Not that I'd expected him to explain.

When we arrived at the top floor, the reception-ist escorted me through the double doors and into an office where I saw Jessica sitting behind a desk.

"Ali, good, you're here."

She stood and led me down a hallway to a closed door. "You'll have to wait out here," she said to Buck, who nodded.

Money was waiting inside, but not where Buck could've seen him.

"How are you doing?" he asked, motioning to the empty sleeve of my coat.

"Better. The pain meds knocked me for a loop for a few days."

He helped me with my coat and draped it over an empty chair. "Have a seat."

I waited until both he and Jessica were seated before speaking. "As I said earlier, I believe someone is trying to kill Sumner Copeland."

Money rested his elbows on the table and steepled his fingers in front of his mouth. "I've also received a request to put him on paid leave, pending an investigation."

"I thought he was already on leave?"

Money nodded.

"Do you know who's targeting him?"

"The edict came directly from the director."

"Fisk?"

"Affirmative."

Like in Cope's apartment, I couldn't sit still. I stood and paced. "Why?" My question was rhetorical. If Money knew, he would've said already. "What do you want me to do now?" There was no point in my continuing with my original mission. If Cope was dirty, he'd be arrested, not murdered.

"Stay the course. He knows who's targeting him and why. It'll be up to you to find out."

I grabbed my coat and was about to walk out when Money's phone buzzed at the same time Jessica's did.

"Yes," he answered, holding up one finger when I put my hand on the door.

I looked at Jessica, who hadn't answered her phone. She shrugged.

"I'll wait for an update," we both heard Money say. He set his phone on the table and rubbed his eyes. "There was a shooting. Irish is in surgery. There are reports of another casualty. It's unclear who it is."

I pulled open the door, not caring if Buck saw Money. "I need to get back." Buck nodded, and I knew he'd heard. "Where's Cope?"

"On his way to the hospital."

"Take me there."

We raced to the elevator; Buck's phone vibrated. "Wheaton," he answered. "She's right here." I couldn't hear what the person on the other end of the phone was saying. "Copy that." Buck disconnected the call and put the phone in his pocket. "My orders are to escort you back to the apartment."

20

Cope

I grabbed my phone when it vibrated moments after I ended my call with Buck.

"Cope. I just heard," said Decker. "Any word on his condition?"

"I'm headed to the hospital now." I didn't want to know, but I had to ask. "Who's down, Deck?"

"Easy."

"Fuck." I had half a mind to turn the car around and drive straight to Langley. Before I killed the Director of the CIA with my bare hands, I needed to get a better read on Irish's condition.

John "Easy" Harris was a former agent. He was married with two kids. Two kids who were now fatherless. Someone was going to fucking pay. Not just for his life but for the lives lost of the other agents all over the world.

Irish had nobody. His parents had both passed in the last few years, and like me, he had no siblings. Didn't even have cousins. I was the closest thing he had to a relative, and I considered him my brother.

I pulled up in front of the same hospital Ali had been taken to, tossed the rental's keys to the waiting valet, and raced inside.

"Surgery?" I asked as I ran past the information desk.

"Fourth floor but, sir…"

I was inside the elevator before the woman finished her sentence. It opened to another desk.

"Can I help you?"

"Paxon Warrick." I turned my head and saw Rage waiting.

"Your name?"

"Sumner Copeland."

"Someone will be out to speak with you as soon as there's something to report."

Rage stood when I approached. "Sorry, Cope."

"Not your fault. Who else was in there with you?"

"Ink. He's working it from the inside."

I nodded and walked over to the windows. "What happened?" I asked when Rage was close enough that we could speak without anyone overhearing.

"Cellblock ambush."

"Who was the shooter?"

"There were two. Both guards."

"Did you recognize them?"

"Negative. First time I'd seen either of them."

"Excuse me," I said when my cell rang with a call from my father. "Dad."

"Where are you?"

"At Saint James' Hospital."

"I'm on my way."

"Dad, you don't need to—"

A little over an hour later, he walked off the elevator and motioned for me to follow him down a corridor. He pushed open the door of the chapel.

"What the fuck have you and Irish gotten yourselves mixed up in?" His face was beet red.

"Have a seat, Dad."

He glared at me.

"Have a seat, and I'll tell you."

He walked to the front pew and sat; I remained standing.

"The first thing you need to know is that Warrick is innocent."

"Get on with the rest of it."

"Not until you swear on my life that you'll let me finish what I've started."

"Absolutely not."

"Then, I won't tell you a fucking thing." I turned to stalk out.

"Sumner. Wait. I'll swear to it."

"Sit back down."

I'd just finished telling my father about the mission Irish and I took on without authorization from anyone within the agency or the committee that oversaw it, when my phone buzzed with a message from Rage.

"He's out of surgery." I bolted out of the chapel and back to the waiting area.

"Mr. Copeland?"

"Yes."

"I'm Dr. Pollari, the head trauma surgeon. Mr. Warrick is out of surgery and is being transferred to the SICU. He suffered several body cavity GSW, the main damage to left renal, pancreas, and spleen."

"When can I see him?"

"Give it another hour or two. Register with the surgical ICU. They'll contact you when you can go in."

"What's his condition?"

"Still critical."

I turned when the doctor walked away, and met my father's eyes. "I'm sorry, son. We're all praying."

The elevator doors opened, and Ali stepped out, followed by both Rock and Buck. When I looked into her beautiful eyes, I felt a sense of relief that even my father hadn't given me. She put one arm around me, and I held her close.

"You were supposed to wait at the apartment," I murmured, breathing in the scent of her hair.

"I couldn't."

I pulled back, cupped her cheek with my palm, and looked into her tear-filled eyes.

"How is he?"

"Still critical, but alive." I felt a hand squeeze my shoulder.

"This must be Miss Graham," said my father.

"Ali, this is my dad."

"Nice to meet you, Mr. Copeland." I loved that she didn't let go of me to shake my father's hand.

"Call me Henry."

"If you will all excuse us," I said, leading Ali toward the chapel where my father and I had talked. "I'll deal with you two later," I muttered to Buck and Rock when we walked past them.

"Don't blame them," Ali said when I opened the door and motioned for her to go inside.

"Should've been two against one." I winked and she smiled. "Ali…"

She shook her head. "Don't, Cope."

"What do you mean?"

"Whatever you're about to tell me, don't."

I sat on the pew where my father had and pulled her down next to me. "Why not?"

"Not yet." She put her arm around my waist and rested her head on my shoulder. "I had to see you."

I ran my hand through her hair. "I'm sorry I told Buck not to let you come."

"I understand."

"Do you?" I said, putting my fingers under her chin and raising her head so I could see her eyes.

"Will Warrick be okay?"

"I believe he will." I heard the door open and the distinct sound of my father clearing his throat. I turned my head.

"Just need a minute, Sumner."

"Be right back."

I followed him out into the corridor. "As soon as Irish can be moved, I've made arrangements to have him relocated to an undisclosed location."

"Dad, I asked you—"

He held up his hand. "No one within the agency will have any idea where he is."

"No one?"

"No one, son. Executive order."

"Thanks, Dad."

"I'm assuming you have your own team to put in place as far as protection, but if you need help, I can make a couple of calls."

"Does the president know?"

My father shook his head. "I've been around a long time, Sumner, and I don't ask for very many favors."

"Thank you," I said, hugging him.

"I'd do anything for you, son. Anything."

As I watched him walk away, I wondered if I should've gone to him years ago when all this began. I'd been so afraid to trust anyone that I'd lost sight of the fact that there were people who had earned it.

21

Ali

While I sat in the apartment, worried sick about Cope, I'd come to a decision. There was enough evidence piling up that neither Cope nor Irish were the moles. I didn't know who was yet, but it wasn't my job to figure that out.

I called Money directly, and he accepted my suggestion that there was no need for me to continue my assignment. He offered to inform Jessica.

"Will you be returning to California right away?"

I had planned to stay a few more days, but until that moment, it hadn't occurred to me that the end of the assignment would mean I couldn't stay in the apartment any longer. "I'm not sure, but I can move my stuff out of the apartment this evening."

"There's no hurry. You can stay. Just let Jessica know your plans."

I'd thanked him and told him I would.

After I hung up, I realized I had no idea which hospital Irish was in. Instead of calling Money back, I opened my front door.

"We can do this one of two ways. You can take me to wherever Cope is, or I'll go above your heads and do it." I took out my identification—my real identification—and showed it to them. "My reason for wanting to go to him is entirely personal and has nothing to do with my job. He has enough on his mind right now. Do not burden him with this." I looked into both Buck's and Rock's eyes, and they nodded.

Now here I sat, knowing Cope had been about to confess all to me a few minutes ago, but I wasn't ready to do the same. I wanted one more night with him. I wouldn't ask for more than that.

"They said I can see him now," Cope said from the chapel doorway.

I brushed away the tear that fell, and stood. "Go ahead. I'll wait here for you."

"I won't be long. They said I can only stay fifteen minutes."

I nodded and waved and then sat back down on the pew. Cope looked so hopeful. As though whatever weight he'd been carrying was about to be lifted. And maybe it was. I hoped so for his sake.

"Mom," I whispered, standing to light a candle on the altar. "If you can hear me, I need you and Dad to look out for him. He's a good man."

"And you love him," I heard a woman's voice say.

I turned around and saw Stella sitting in the back pew. "How long have you been here?"

"Just a minute or two." She got up and walked toward me. "Sounds like you're leavin', sis. You gonna say goodbye first?"

I shrugged a shoulder. "He has a lot going on."

"So you're just gonna walk out the door and break his heart? Is that your plan, Ali Graham Mancuso?"

"My assignment is over. No point in sticking around."

"No explanation? No nothing?"

"I was assigned to determine whether Cope was Irish's accomplice. He may have been, but not in the way anyone originally believed."

"Have a seat." Stella pointed to the front pew.

"I should be going."

"Have a seat," she repeated, standing between me and the door. "I have a story to tell you." When I sat down on the pew opposite the one she'd pointed to, she laughed. "That'll do." She walked up to the altar and lit the candle next to the one I had. "I'm a little older than you," she began. "But you and I have something in common."

"What's that?"

"We're both in love with Sumner Copeland. Wanna know what we don't have in common?"

I nodded, willing my eyes not to fill with tears.

"Cope doesn't love me."

"He doesn't know who I really am."

"Do you really think that's going to make a difference?"

"I do. Besides, assignment's over, like I said. Time for me to go home."

"If he asks, what do you want me to tell him?"

"I'm not going to ask you to lie, if that's what you think."

"I did some digging. You're a good writer, Jennifer Cavalleri. You could be a damn good reporter."

"How'd you know it was me?"

"I already am a damn good reporter. One of the best, in fact. So, why'd you quit?"

"The CIA made me an offer that was hard to turn down."

"I read your book. It was really good."

The book Stella referenced was an exposé on rampant corruption in the State of Illinois. I'd written it while I was still at Northwestern and hadn't known at the time that the department chair of the school of journalism, a woman who was also my mentor, had sent the manuscript off to an editor she knew at one of the remaining big five publishing houses. By the time they offered me a contract, I was already employed by the CIA. It didn't thrill me that Stella had linked me to it, since the publisher guaranteed there would be no link to me and that's what I'd assured the agency.

"Hey, Stella. I didn't know you were here," said Cope, coming in the chapel door.

"Just keepin' Ali company while she waits. How's Irish?"

"They said he looks a lot worse than he is, but they believe he's going to pull through."

"I'd ask you for an exclusive, but my guess is Ali will get it before I do."

Cope rested his hands on the back of the pew. "It isn't over yet, Stella."

She nodded, and I wasn't sure how I'd missed it before. It was so obvious now that she was in love with him. I wondered if Cope knew.

He held out his hand to me. "Ready to go home, baby?"

My eyes met Stella's, and I waited. "Have a good night, you two." I stood, and she followed us out to where Buck and Rock waited.

Cope pulled me back into the corridor. "I want you to ride back with the guys. There's one more thing I have to take care of tonight. I'll meet you at my apartment."

When he bent down and kissed me, I wrapped my right arm around his neck. "Don't be too long," I whispered.

"When I get there, I want you in bed, naked. Understood?"

"Understood."

He started to walk away, but then turned back and pushed me up against the wall. "There's something I need to tell you."

"Tell me when you get home."

He shook his head. "I can't wait."

"Cope—"

He cupped my cheek with his palm. "I love you, Ali."

I asked to sit in the back of the car on the ride back and sat up when I saw the sign for the Civil War Museum, remembering how animated Cope had gotten when he told me about it. "My grandfather used to take me there a lot," he said. "Often, we spent more time outside, sitting on one of the benches while he told me stories, than we did inside."

We'd just pulled into the parking garage when both Rock's and Buck's cells went off. Buck answered his. I could only see the back of his head, but somehow I knew, whatever the call was about, was bad.

"Come on upstairs," said Rock with his arm around my shoulders. Buck was still inside the car, on this phone.

"What's going on?" I asked once we were in the elevator.

"I don't know."

"Then, why are you and Buck acting so strangely?"

"I'll see what I can find out once you're settled."

When I pulled my phone out of my pocket, Rock took it out of my hand. "What the fuck? Give that back to me."

"Ali—"

"You know who I am, Rock. Give me my goddamn phone."

The elevator door opened on the thirtieth floor, and Rock took my arm. "Come on. Just do this for me."

I let him lead me inside. With every step, the sick feeling in my stomach grew more intense. The door closed behind us.

"Ali, sit down."

"No."

"Please."

"Something's happened to Cope, hasn't it?"

He didn't answer.

"Just fucking tell me, Rock. What happened?"

I raced over, grabbed the television remote, and turned it on before he could stop me. I sunk to my knees as I watched the report.

"A car exploded in the parking lot of Saint James' Hospital at approximately seven this evening. Reports indicate one fatality."

Behind the reporter, I could see the whirling red lights of the emergency vehicles that surrounded the burned-out shell of the car I knew was Cope's rental.

22

Ali

The next three days were a blur. Chloe flew in and stayed with me in Cope's apartment. Rock and Buck were still there, along with other operatives they worked with. There were six apartments on the thirtieth floor of the building, and they all seemed to be occupied by people they were affiliated with.

Whenever someone came to the door, Chloe spoke with them. The only people she let in to see me were Stella and Lindsey from the café downstairs.

I sat and listened while they spoke to me, but after they left, I couldn't remember what they'd said.

"How are you doing?" Chloe asked when I came out of Cope's bedroom and found her sitting at the kitchen counter. It seemed that no matter what time of day or night it was, that's where I found her.

"I should go home."

"We can do that, but don't you want to stay for the service?"

"Service?"

"The memorial service, sweetie."

"I...I...can't," I stammered, gripping the back of the kitchen stool.

Chloe got up and put her arms around me. "You don't have to. We can go home. Tonight, if that's what you want."

"I do." I couldn't imagine facing Cope's parents. Or people wondering who the woman was who could barely hold herself together. "I have to go home."

"I'll make the arrangements." She turned to go down the hallway to the guest bedroom.

"Chloe?"

"Yeah, sweetie?"

"Have you heard from them?" She'd been answering my cell phone. In fact, I didn't even know where it was.

"Who?"

"Cope's parents?"

She came back over and brushed the hair from my forehead. "I haven't."

I bent at the waist and buried my head on my arm that rested on the back of the stool, crying so hard my stomach hurt. I closed my eyes, imagining it was

Cope's fingers rather than my friend's moving my hair from my face.

Chloe rubbed my back with her hand. "Do you want me to see if I can get in touch with them?"

I raised my head and brushed at my tears. "I just want to go home."

"Then, that's what we'll do."

When someone knocked on the door, I went back to the bedroom and threw myself on the bed, trying my damnedest not to feel sorry for myself. Cope was the one who was dead. Him, my mother, and my father. I looked up at the ceiling. "I swear, if you take Chloe from me…"

What? I was threatening God now? I couldn't help it; she was the only person left I cared about.

I heard Chloe's footsteps headed my way and sat up. "There's someone here who wants to talk to you."

"Who is it?"

"His name is Decker Ashford."

When I went back to the kitchen, Buck was waiting with the man I assumed was Ashford. Buck came over and hugged me like he always did.

"How are you holding up?"

I shook my head, knowing that if I answered, I'd start crying again.

"I understand. Listen, there's someone I want you to meet. Ali, this is Decker. He's my boss and a good friend of Cope's."

"Hi," was the best I could muster.

"I'll make our reservations," said Chloe when Decker asked me to sit with him, and Buck walked in the direction of the front door.

"What reservations?" I heard Buck ask her.

"Ali wants to go home," she answered.

"When?"

"As soon as I can get a flight."

From where I sat, I could see Buck make eye contact with Decker, who nodded.

"I'll take care of it," he said.

"Um…okay," said Chloe, walking back over to us. "I mean, I can do it."

Decker shook his head. "Do you want to leave tonight or in the morning?"

Could I leave tonight? I wasn't sure I could stand not spending one more night in Cope's bed, knowing that it would be the last time I ever would. "Tomorrow," I whispered.

Decker leaned forward and rested his elbows on his knees. "I've known Cope for a really long time. He was a good friend."

I nodded, wishing I could get up, go back to the bedroom, and not listen to him. I didn't want to talk about him. I wanted him to walk through the door, put his arms around me, and tell me it was all a terrible mistake.

"I'm sorry," I said, standing and rushing down the hallway.

I don't know how much time had passed when Chloe came into the bedroom. "Ali, Mr. Ashford is still here. I'm sorry, but he said it's important he speak with you."

I rolled over and sat up. "Okay."

I followed her back out to the kitchen and apologized to the man still sitting in the living room area.

"I understand, and if it weren't imperative we speak, I wouldn't bother you. I know you had deep feelings for Cope and he, you."

I nodded, wishing he'd get to the point.

"I know who you are, Ali, and what you do."

"Yes. I assumed you did by now."

"The mission isn't over. Does that make sense to you?"

"How is Irish?"

"He's recovering and has been moved to an undisclosed location for his protection."

I took a deep breath and let it out slowly.

"You also remain in danger. Until this is all over, you will need protection too."

"Why?"

"Because whoever Cope and Irish were investigating believes you know more than you do. The night your apartment was broken into, was evidence of that. Until we determine who that is, whether it's one or many people, you'll remain under protection."

"Who knows this?"

"Your chain of command along with Money McTiernan."

"Anyone else?"

"It's need to know, Ali."

"Okay."

"Buck will be traveling with you. He'll be staying with you as well, at your house. He won't be the only agent on your detail. There will be others, who remain at the covert level of surveillance."

"Understood, sir."

The man reached forward and covered my hand with his. "Decker is my name, and you don't work for me, Ali. We're here for you. Just let us know what else you need."

"When can I leave?"

"Whenever you'd like. There's a plane on standby."

"I'd like to go now." It didn't matter if I stayed one more night. Tomorrow I'd feel the same way, and the day after.

He nodded his head in a way that suggested he wasn't surprised.

"Just give me a few minutes to get your stuff together," said Chloe from where she stood in the kitchen.

"I can do it." By the time I got to the bedroom, Chloe was wheeling my bag out. "I'll just need a minute."

"Take all the time you need."

I sat on the bed and hugged the pillow close to me. "I wish I would've told you I loved you too, Cope. Because I do," I whispered. "I know it doesn't make sense, but it's true. I wish we'd had more time together, but I've asked my parents to look out for you, wherever you all are. I'll love you forever, Sumner Copeland."

I wiped my tears and took one last look around the room I'd only spent a couple of nights in, yet it seemed I'd spent a lifetime.

"I'm ready."

"Do you want me to help you change, sweetie?" asked Chloe.

I shook my head. I'd been wearing Cope's sweatshirt and had no intention of taking it off.

23

Ali

One Month Later

"What are you working on?" asked Buck, joining me in the kitchen.

"Just writing." I'd gotten my cast off the day before, and it felt so good to be able to type without having a rolled-up towel under my wrist.

"I'm glad you didn't need surgery," he said, pouring himself a cup of coffee.

My arm had healed quickly and, as Buck had said, didn't need further care. It ached, but my heart hurt worse. There were days I couldn't bear it, and others, I was able to set my grief aside.

I didn't know the whole story yet, but I knew enough to start the book I was aware would never be published, but was one I had to write anyway.

Irish hadn't resurfaced, but Buck reported he had recovered fully. He didn't need to tell me the mission Warrick and Cope were working wasn't over. As long as Buck and the other agents were here, it meant it remained unresolved.

"Anything you want to do today?"

I shook my head. It was too difficult to do much other than stay at home.

The last few days, Buck and I had worked in the small garden he'd cleared the way for in the backyard of the house that had belonged to my parents and had been mine since my mother's death. It was the house I grew up in, and when I'd showed Buck photos of how it looked when my father was still alive, he asked me if I wanted to have a vegetable garden like the one in the pictures.

I loved the idea, and while he tilled the soil, I worked on cleaning up some of the other beds that had once been filled with flowers.

The rose bushes were very overgrown and what I planned to tackle today. I'd been working on trimming and shaping them when I noticed Buck studying his phone.

He looked up, and his eyes met mine. "There's been an arrest."

"Who?"

"Fisk."

Dizziness overtook me, and I grabbed a hold of the split-rail fence. "The director?"

Buck nodded. "Come on, let's get you inside before you pass out on me."

I sat down on the sofa and took a sip of the glass of water Buck brought me.

"There isn't a lot of information available yet, but I'm sure that will change in the next few days."

"You can go home now."

He shrugged. "I kinda like it here."

I smiled. We had settled into an easy rhythm of day-to-day life. Buck gave me space to mourn Cope, especially on the days when I couldn't seem to think about anything else and wallowed in my sorrow. He'd been gone longer than I'd known him, but that didn't change how much I felt his absence from my life. Writing his story, brought him back to me, at least a little.

I hoped that, once it was all over, I could get in touch with Irish and that he'd tell me what the world, and I, would never know otherwise.

My cell vibrated on the kitchen counter, and Buck walked it over to me. "It's Stella."

"Has Buck told you?" she asked.

"A few minutes ago."

"Shit is going to hit the fucking fan. This is big, Ali. I'll send you everything I can."

"I appreciate it." It was Stella who'd suggested I write Cope's story. "If nothing else, it'll be therapeutic," she'd said.

I'd just ended the call with her when Chloe called. "It's all over the news. The Director of the CIA was arrested this morning."

"I heard."

"Do you think this has anything to do with Cope?"

"I do."

"I hope this means closure, Al."

"Me too." I wished that meant the ever-present ache in my chest would begin to diminish. I knew better, though. While it didn't hurt as bad, the same pain was present whenever I thought about my parents too.

"Do you want some time alone?" Buck asked when I set the phone down.

"No. Better to keep busy." I followed him out to the yard and went back to pruning my roses. *"Shit!"* I muttered a few minutes later when the pruning shears slipped and I cut my finger.

"What happened?" Buck asked, rushing over to me. "Let me see," he said, grasping my right wrist. He pulled the bandanna from around his neck, wrapped it around my finger, and put pressure on it. "Let's get you inside and get it cleaned up. You might need stitches."

"It's just a cut, Buck."

He lowered one of his fatherly gazes on me, and I let him lead me inside. We walked through the back door, and the hair on the back of my neck stood on end. I could feel someone else's presence in my house.

As we rounded the corner, I looked up into the most beautiful green eyes I'd ever seen. "Cope?" I whispered right before I fainted.

24

Cope

Thirty-five days ago, I did one of the hardest things I'd ever had to do, and got in a car that would whisk me away from the hospital where I told the woman I believed was my soulmate that I loved her.

"You keep her safe," I said to Decker countless times on the drive from there to the airfield that would take me to the place where I'd stay until it was safe for me to come out of hiding. Or until my location was compromised and I'd be forced to move.

The small house sat across the bay from where I knew Ali lived and where she was being protected from harm.

I didn't know for sure whether anyone would come after her, but I couldn't take any chances. When this was finally all over, I just hoped she'd forgive me for what I'd had no choice but to do.

"There's something you need to know," Decker had said to me that night.

"Is it about Ali?"

"Yes."

"Decker, I—"

"No, Cope. You need to know."

When he told me Ali worked for the Internal Affairs Division of the United States Inspector General, I wasn't surprised. It was the only element of the CIA created separately by statute that had obligations to both the agency and to Congress and was responsible for overseeing accountability in the management of CIA activities by performing independent investigations of programs and operations when necessary.

It took me a few days to process that news, but in my gut, I didn't believe it had only been about the job for her. Ali cared for me. I sensed it deep in my soul. Part of me hoped she loved me as much as I loved her, but I wouldn't know that until the day came when I could finally look into her ocean eyes and ask.

Decker kept me abreast of her as well as Irish, who had recovered fully and was also being guarded in a safe, undisclosed location.

While Ali had been permitted to stay in her home, the level of security protecting her was unprecedented and had been arranged by my father, who I spoke with at least once every few days.

He'd put the full force of the United States Senate Select Committee on Intelligence behind the investigation into the mole that had been selling secrets to the Chinese for almost a decade and who had been responsible for the deaths of dozens of agents, operatives, and assets.

In the end, as I'd expected, it wasn't one man, but many, who made up the network of double-agents, all of whom had been arrested in a carefully planned and executed manner. The arrests had been made around the world simultaneously; in the case of the US, it had been in the middle of the night.

"It's over, son," my father said when I answered his call at four this morning.

"I need to be certain, Dad."

"I understand. The brief is on its way to you."

I'd read it again and again, pouring over every detail, making sure every question I'd had was answered. Only then did I ask Ink, one of the men who had been on my duty for the last month, to take me across the bay.

Rock approached when the car pulled up in front of her house. "They're in the backyard," he told me before opening the door to let me inside.

I stood and watched her from a window, and what I saw, broke my heart. Gone was my little spitfire, and in her place was a woman in pain. It was etched all over her face and in the way her shoulders drooped forward.

My hand was on the door to go out when I heard her cry out and saw she'd cut her finger. As if in slow motion, I watched Buck race over to her. When he led in her my direction, I went back into the living room.

I stood silently, waiting for her to notice me, hating that Buck's arm was around her, until she finally raised her eyes and stared into mine.

"Cope?" she whispered. I saw her eyes roll back in her head and her knees buckle. I raced over and caught her in my arms even though Buck had been closer.

"She has a cut on her hand," he said as I carried her over to the sofa and sat with her on my lap. I nodded, and Buck walked out the front door, closing it behind him.

"Ali, my love," I murmured, brushing her hair from her face. When her eyes opened, I bent my head and kissed her. "Hi," I said when her eyes filled with tears.

"Cope?" she repeated.

"I'm really here, Ali, and I'm so sorry."

What began as a few tears, turned into sobs as we clung to each other.

"I'd hoped," she whispered.

"I wish I could've told you, warned you, but I couldn't."

All the muscles in her body tensed as she wriggled out of my arms. She wiped her tears with her left hand that was no longer covered by a cast, and stood.

"There's something I need to tell you."

"I already know."

She studied me, and I held my hand out to her. "Come back. My arms ache not holding you."

"You're not angry?"

"When did it stop being a job for you, Ali?"

She smiled, her cheeks turned pink, and she finally took my hand and let me pull her back on my lap. I grasped the back of her neck and kissed her. It felt unbelievably good when she wrapped *both* arms around my neck.

"Well?" I asked, pulling back and looking into her eyes.

"I think it was the baklava that did it."

I raised a brow, remembering her swatting the back of my hand with a fork.

"Or maybe it was when I woke up after the accident and you were sitting beside me."

"You almost died because of me," I murmured, closing my mind to the memory of when I first saw my car and realized how close she'd come.

"I didn't, though. Neither did you," she said, cupping my cheek like I'd done so many times to her. "I love you."

"Say it again."

"I love you, Sumner Copeland."

"I love you too, Ali Graham Mancuso."

25

Ali

One Month Later

"You're sure about this?" Cope asked as we walked toward the two exercise bikes that sat near the floor-to-ceiling windows of his loft.

"I did it yesterday with the drapes closed. Today I'll try with them open."

"Keep your eyes on the floor," he murmured, holding my hand until I was on the seat of the bike. He'd turned it on earlier and had it set up so I could see him in a window on the screen once he was on the one beside me.

The workout he'd programmed started slow, but as competitive as we both were, I knew that soon we'd enter race mode.

"Look up, baby," he said.

"I will."

"I know you can do it."

I slowly raised my head and looked in front of me. All I could see was the building across the street. "So far so good," I told him.

"Now look at me."

I turned my head, but stopped when I saw the view of the Capitol Building. "It really is breathtaking," I murmured.

"Sure is."

I turned to Cope, who was looking at me rather than out the window.

"I'm proud of you, Ali."

"I'm proud of me too." I turned back to the screen when I felt the tension in the pedals tighten.

"Ready?" he asked.

"Bring it."

He won the virtual race, of course, but I didn't mind, because I'd won something too. I couldn't say that every time I got near the windows, or in the elevator, or any other place where my fear of heights once crippled me, that it wouldn't be a struggle. But today, I'd conquered those fears enough to something that I sometimes felt was more important to Cope than it was to me.

Later this evening, we were having dinner at his parents' house, like we did every Sunday. Since we were celebrating Fisk receiving three life sentences after his conviction earlier this week, Cope had invited several of the men who had protected both of us through the final days of the mission that had begun so many years before. I couldn't wait to see Buck, who had become like a brother to me. I'm sure Cope felt the same about seeing Irish.

"Hey," said Cope, looking at his phone while I made us both coffee. "Stella said she's going to be able to make it after all."

I was anxious to talk to her about the book we'd been working on together—working title, *Two Spies Who Took Down the Mole.* Cope balked at the name, but I loved it. Ultimately, it would be up to the publisher to decide, if the book even got picked up. Something told me it would, though.

"We have some celebrating to do tonight," Cope said when he climbed behind me in the tub that was almost identical to the one in the apartment I'd been staying in when we met. "I think we should start now, though."

"You won't get any argument from me." I took his right hand and put it on my breast. When I reached for his left hand, he had it above his head.

"Close your eyes," he whispered into my ear before nipping its lobe. "Are they closed?"

"Yes."

26

Cope

I'd had it since the week after Fisk was arrested and I knew Ali and I would be free to live our lives without fear. I also knew by then that she loved me as much as I loved her.

"Open," I said, holding a box in front of her. When she gasped, I bent my neck and kissed the side of her face. "Will you marry me, Ali?"

"Yes," she whispered, making me regret I hadn't done this in a way that I could see her face.

I slid the ring on the third finger of her left hand. It was a perfect fit.

I set the box on the floor when she scooted away from me, got on her knees, and turned around. There were tears in her eyes, but she was smiling. I pulled her toward me and kissed her hard. "I love you so fucking much."

She stood and pulled me up with her. Dripping from the bath, we padded our way into the bedroom. When she rested against the pillows, I kissed my way from her lips down her body, stopping first at her breasts and then again when I reached the apex between her legs.

"Cope?"

I raised my head and looked into her eyes.

"Make love to me."

I licked my way back up her body and kissed her. I understood what she wanted. I wanted it too. I rested my elbows on either side of her neck and entered her slowly. My eyes met hers; I didn't want to do as much as blink.

"I love you," she said, as I began to move.

I rotated my hips, my cock filling her warmth, exploring, like I did with my tongue.

"Ali." It was too much for me to hold back.

Her neck arched, and she met my thrusts.

"You're mine," I groaned as I came.

"And you're mine."

We'd been to my parents' house for dinner every Sunday we were in DC rather than at Ali's house in California. Tonight would be different, though. Our friends would be there too, giving me the chance to tell those who meant the most to me, that Ali had agreed to become my wife.

"Ready?" I asked when I pulled up to the door. Several cars were lining the street in front of the house.

Ali was studying her engagement ring. "Did I tell you how much I love it?"

"Maybe twenty or thirty times."

While I grabbed the box of champagne we'd brought with us, Ali carried the vase of flowers she always brought my mother when we visited. The second time she'd done so, I told her it wasn't necessary: my parents had beautiful gardens.

"I don't feel right arriving empty-handed, Cope," she told me. "It isn't polite."

I smiled then, and now, remembering how Ali had said she didn't feel right, using a restaurant's restroom without purchasing something. She'd bought me a piece of pie that morning, and shortly after, another vehicle had rammed into my car while she was driving it.

When I reached for the door's handle, Ali covered my hand with hers. I raised my brow and looked into her eyes.

"Happy memories today, Cope."

"Happy memories," I murmured in answer.

It was uncanny how my future wife always seemed to notice when I thought about how I'd almost lost her, sometimes before I even realized I was thinking about it.

When I opened the door, I was stunned to see the living room just off the entryway was full. All of the people we'd expected to come, were there, along with many more we hadn't anticipated seeing.

Along with Buck and Rock, Decker Ashford and the other Invincibles' partners were there as were the team from another covert ops firm I'd worked with many times called K19 Security Solutions. I'd made sure Chloe could be here too, and loved the look of surprise on Ali's face when she was the first person whose arms she ran into.

"We're likely to start a bidding war," said Kade Butler, founding partner of K19, when he stepped forward to shake my hand.

"He's already ours," said Decker Ashford.

Ali must've overheard the conversation and walked over to put her arm in mine. "He's mine, Decker. All mine."

"We'd be interested in both of you coming on board," said Merrigan, Kade's wife, former MI6 agent, and managing partner of K19. "However, I understand we're celebrating a book release today." Merrigan's eyes focused on Ali's ring finger. "That's not all we're celebrating."

"Shh," Ali whispered. "We haven't told Cope's parents yet."

Merrigan smiled and nodded, clapping her hands in excitement.

"Speaking of my parents." I didn't see either of them.

Ali took my hand and led me into the kitchen, where we found my mom and dad. I deposited the case of champagne I'd had under my arm on the counter.

"There they are," said my father, rushing over to hug Ali and then me. My mother was right behind him.

"What's this?" he asked, pointing to the box.

"We have something extra to celebrate tonight."

Ali thrust her hand, which had been behind her back, in my mother's direction. She gasped, and her eyes filled with tears. My dad patted me on the back, his eyes misty like my mom's were.

"We'd hoped this would happen soon," my mom murmured, hugging Ali for the second time.

"We're so happy for you," said my dad, hugging me a second time too.

I heard someone behind me clear his throat and turned to see Irish in the doorway. The man was the closest thing I'd ever had to a brother.

"Here's the best man, now," I said, motioning for him to join us.

"Seriously?" he asked, putting his arm around Ali's shoulders. "Let me see that thing."

The rest of the evening was filled with endless celebration. My mother was busy first telling Ali the wedding could be whatever she wanted, and then asking how soon she wanted to start planning it. I'd warned her that since I had no siblings, let alone sisters, my mom might overwhelm her when it came to our ceremony. "You're her only daughter. She'll want to spoil you."

"It's okay, Cope. She's my only mother."

Epilogue

Cope

My eyes filled with tears as I watched the woman who would soon be my wife walk down the garden path in my parents' backyard. Ali's arm was tucked in my father's, who had offered to walk her down the aisle. She had ecstatically accepted.

My eyes met Lindsey's, who was standing a couple of rows back. She smiled and winked, perhaps remembering the fateful night when Ali and I met in her café. The same café that, much to my mother's initial shock, was catering the lunch that followed the ceremony.

Ali had requested two things: gyro salad and baklava; otherwise, she gave Lindsey free rein.

"That's odd," my mother had said when she looked at the menu Lindsey had prepared. "But whatever Ali wants, Ali gets. She makes you so happy, Sumner. I will spend my life thanking her for that." She did make me happy. More than I dreamed possible.

Irish put his hand on my shoulder. "She's beautiful," he murmured.

I reached up and covered his hand with mine, so thankful he was alive to stand beside me.

"Only good memories," I could hear Ali say inside my head.

"You both deserve every bit of happiness life brings you."

"So do you, Irish."

"I'm workin' on it. Looks like I'm not the only one." He motioned with his head, and I looked briefly at where Buck stood next to Stella, his arm draped around her shoulders.

My gaze then met my bride's. "I love you," I mouthed. My father lifted her veil, took her hand, and put it in mine.

Keep reading for a sneak peek at
the next book in Heather Slade's
Protector's Undercover Team One series,
Undercover Savior

One stealthy sniper.
One determined reporter.
And the dangerous story that unfolds…

SAVIOR

I'll save them all, or die trying. Our world is riddled with crime, corruption, and evil, and it's my job to keep the innocent safe. But when my childhood friend, my first crush, becomes the target, and her life is in danger, nobody can stop me from protecting her.

SULLIVAN

It was a second, a glimpse into my past, and I could never forget those eyes. Asher Kendricks was my best friend, my confidante, my everything. and now, he just may be my savior as well. However, he's not talking, but someone will. As a reporter, I get the scoop, unearth the secrets. I may be some assassin's target, but there's no way I'm not getting to the bottom of all of this. And when I uncover the secrets, the world will know the truth.

1

Savior

"Take the shot as soon as you've got it," I heard through my comms earpiece. If I wouldn't lose my sights by rolling my eyes, that's what I'd be doing. *Take the shot as soon as I've got it?* Who the fuck did this newbie think he was talking to?

I was one of the best snipers in Unit 23. Not one of—*the* best. I took the shot when I knew I'd take the assailant down.

"Savior? Copy?"

"Shut the fuck up," I seethed, pulling the trigger the very instant I knew I'd hit the bastard right between the eyes. There might be a little blood splatter on the woman he was attempting to use as a human shield, but she'd live. He wouldn't.

A quick *pfft* was all he heard. It might not have even registered. No crack since I only used sub-sonic bullets. Once he was on the ground, the clean-up crew moved in. One for him. One to get the woman to safety.

"Wait!" I heard a female voice call out, but I kept going. I came in, got rid of the bad guy, and someone else handled the rest. I didn't do victims.

I picked up my pace when I heard footfalls getting closer. Periscope, the handler, fucking better stop this woman before she got any closer to me or there'd be bloody hell to pay later.

Her hand landed on my arm just as I reached for the vehicle's door handle and I froze.

"I wanted to thank you—wait, *Asher*?"

I stared into the eyes of the girl who I took to a school dance a lifetime ago. Sullivan Rivers. It was a good damn thing I hadn't known it was her the motherfucker held between himself and certain death. If I had, things might've gone differently. I couldn't say whether I would've risked taking the shot. More likely, I would have ripped the man apart with my bare hands.

"Asher?" she repeated, her eyes boring into mine.

"Sorry, Sav—" Thankfully, Periscope caught herself before revealing my code name. At least she was one for two. Letting Sullivan get close to me would get her written up, maybe even removed from the unit.

I jerked my arm away when Sullivan rested her hand on it. "Sorry, lady. Wrong guy."

I got in the SUV as Periscope led her away. I didn't risk removing my full-face ski mask even with the blacked-out windows, until I was sure I was far enough away that Sullivan wouldn't catch a glimpse of me.

Even if she had, I looked nothing like the scrawny boy she once knew. I'd grown taller, body filled out, and my facial hair finally came in. The other thing that happened between the last time she saw me and now—my heart turned black as coal. That's what happened to people in my line of work. It didn't matter that I was ridding the world of another piece of shit criminal with every bullet I fired. I shot to kill. Period. I lost track of my kill count a long time ago. And yet, they called me Savior.

Keep reading for a sneak peek at
the next book in Heather Slade's
Invincibles Team Two series,
Bucked

***He's a former CIA operative who juggles it all.
She's a hard-core investigative reporter.
Together, they're INVINCIBLE….***

BUCK

Called back to the ranch, after my dad dies, I know I have my work cut out for me. As a CIA operative, I can juggle it all. Always have. Always will. But when she needs my help, I can't possibly refuse. After all, she's the sexiest city slicker, this Buck has ever seen.

STELLA

My heart and soul is in the city. The last place I ever saw myself was on a ranch, getting filthy, and smelling like a barn all day. But I need his help, and he needs mine—whether he realizes it or not. As for him, the most rugged and irresistible man I've ever known, I can make this sacrifice. After all, this city filly could use a BUCK of her own.

1

Buck

"How are you holding up?" I whispered in the ear of the woman standing beside me.

"About as well as you are," she whispered back as we watched the woman I'd fallen hopelessly in love with walk down the aisle toward the man she was marrying instead of me.

My plus-one, Stella, and I had spent a couple of drunken nights drowning in our shared misery since she was equally in love with the groom. I was sure tonight would be no different.

We turned when Ali, the bride, reached Cope, the groom, who stood waiting with the minister who would marry them. It wasn't the bride who captured my gaze, though. It was Stella. She looked so damn pretty today I almost swallowed my tongue when I picked her up at her apartment.

"Stop that," she'd said, punching my arm.

"Stop what?"

"Looking at me like I'm really your date."

I wanted to tell her she really was my date and that she was breathtaking. But I wouldn't put her on the spot like that. The woman, whose real name I didn't know—I'd only heard her referred to as either TJ or Stella—had been in love with Sumner Copeland since the day I met her. It didn't matter that it was unrequited.

Cope had given her the nickname Stella. All the more reason for me not to use it. Maybe today would be the day I stopped. Maybe it would also be the day I told TJ how I really felt about her, and that instead of being her convenient plus-one, I wanted to be the real thing.

I shook my head at my foolishness. Not only would she carry a torch for Cope for-fucking-ever, she was a city girl. Born and raised. I was the exact opposite. I'd grown up on a ranch, shoveling shit, and never able to get the dirt out from under my fingernails.

The thing we had in common, other than being in love with people who weren't in love with us, was that we'd both traveled the world for our jobs.

She was an award-winning journalist, and up until recently, I had been an agent with the CIA. I'd retired but still worked in the business, just for a private intelligence firm instead.

That was how TJ and I met. I'd been assigned to an op involving asset protection—for Ali. TJ was covering a trial involving Cope, during which Ali's safety had been compromised.

I glanced at my date again when the minister began the ceremony. Instead of looking at Cope, she was looking at me.

About the Author

USA Today and Amazon Top 15 Bestselling Author Heather Slade writes shamelessly sexy, edge-of-your seat romantic suspense.

She gave herself the gift of writing a book for her own birthday one year. Fifty-plus books later (and counting), she's having the time of her life.

The women Slade writes are self-confident, strong, with wills of their own, and hearts as big as the Colorado sky. The men are sublimely sexy, seductive alphas who rise to the challenge of capturing the sweet soul of a woman whose heart they'll hold in the palm of their hand forever. Add in a couple of neck-snapping twists and turns, a page-turning mystery, and a swoon-worthy HEA, and you'll be holding one of her books in your hands.

She loves to hear from my readers. You can contact her at heather@heatherslade.com

To keep up with her latest news and releases, please visit her website at www.heatherslade.com to sign up for her newsletter.

MORE FROM AUTHOR HEATHER SLADE

BUTLER RANCH
Kade's Worth
Brodie's Promise
Maddox's Truce
Naughton's Secret
Mercer's Vow
Kade's Return
Butler Ranch Christmas

WICKED WINEMAKERS
FIRST LABEL
Brix's Bid
Ridge's Release
Press' Passion
Zin's Sins
Tryst's Temptation

WICKED WINEMAKERS
SECOND LABEL
Beau's Beloved
Coming Soon:
Cru's Crush
Bones' Bliss
Snapper's Seduction
Kick's Kiss

ROARING FORK RANCH
Coming Soon:
Roaring Fork Wrangler
Roaring Fork Roughstock
Roaring Fork Rockstar
Roaring Fork Rooker
Roaring Fork Bridger

THE ROYAL AGENTS
OF MI6
Make Me Shiver
Drive Me Wilder
Feel My Pinch
Chase My Shadow
Find My Angel

K19 SECURITY
SOLUTIONS TEAM ONE
Razor's Edge
Gunner's Redemption
Mistletoe's Magic
Mantis' Desire
Dutch's Salvation

K19 SECURITY
SOLUTIONS TEAM TWO
Striker's Choice
Monk's Fire
Halo's Oath
Tackle's Honor
Onyx's Awakening

K19 SHADOW OPERATIONS
TEAM ONE
Code Name: Ranger
Code Name: Diesel
Code Name: Wasp
Code Name: Cowboy
Code Name: Mayhem

K19 ALLIED INTELLIGENCE
TEAM ONE
Code Name: Ares
Code Name: Cayman
Code Name: Poseidon
Code Name: Zeppelin
Code Name: Magnet

K19 ALLIED INTELLIGENCE
TEAM TWO
Coming Soon:
Code Name: Puck
Code Name: Michelangelo
Code Name: Typhon
Code Name: Hornet
Code Name: Reaper

PROTECTORS
UNDERCOVER
TEAM ONE
Undercover Agent
Undercover Emissary
Coming Soon:
Undercover Savior
Undercover Infidel
Undercover Assassin

THE INVINCIBLES
TEAM ONE
Decked
Edged
Grinded
Riled
Smoked

THE INVINCIBLES
TEAM TWO
Bucked
Irished
Sainted
Hammered
Ripped

THE UNSTOPPABLES
TEAM ONE
Furied
Merried

COWBOYS OF
CRESTED BUTTE
A Cowboy Falls
A Cowboy's Dance
A Cowboy's Kiss
A Cowboy Stays
A Cowboy Wins